Nat
2/17

# BACK IN THE
# SOLDIER'S ARMS

# BACK IN THE SOLDIER'S ARMS

BY

SORAYA LANE

First published in Great Britain 2012
by Mills & Boon, an imprint of Harlequin (UK) Limited.
Large Print edition 2012
Harlequin (UK) Limited, Eton House,
18-24 Paradise Road, Richmond, Surrey TW9 1SR

© Soraya Lane 2012

ISBN: 978 0 263 22587 7

Harlequin (UK) policy is to use papers that are natural,
renewable and recyclable products and made from
wood grown in sustainable forests. The logging and
manufacturing process conform to the legal environmental
regulations of the country of origin.

Printed and bound in Great Britain
by CPI Antony Rowe, Chippenham, Wiltshire

For my mother, Maureen. There is no possible way I could have written this book without your help. Thank you so much for all the hours and days you spend helping me with Mackenzie—you are always appreciated and very much loved by us both.

# CHAPTER ONE

"Mommy!"

The high-pitched squeal echoed through the overcrowded airport arrivals lounge.

Penny Cartwright dropped her bag to the floor, not caring where it fell. She could have been flying, her feet moving so fast across the ground it was as if she had wings.

"Gabby!" she cried back. "Gabby!"

Her little girl ducked beneath a barrier, brown curls bouncing, the smile on her face so wide it almost broke Penny's heart.

"Mommy!" The scream was louder now.

Penny forgot everything else. The sounds of too many people talking, flights being announced over the speaker—everything. She dropped to her knees, skidded on the floor as her daughter flew into her arms. Her hands gripped Gabby so tight she thought she might have crushed her.

"Mommy, Mommy!"

Penny inhaled the scent of her, closed her eyes as tears fell onto Gabby's soft hair. "I'm here, baby. I'm home."

Her daughter wriggled. "You're hurting me."

Penny slackened her grip, laughing as tears started to roll down her cheeks, curling down to her mouth. She didn't try to stop them. After all these months, these were happy tears. The kind she didn't mind shedding. The kind she'd been looking forward to shedding.

"You know what?"

Gabby gazed up at her. "What?"

Big brown eyes looked into Penny's, open and trusting. *Loving.*

"You're even more beautiful than the last time I saw you."

Gabby giggled. "Didn't you have a photo of me at work?"

Penny sighed. She'd always called it *work* to her daughter, wanting what she did to sound normal. Not wanting her to know how dangerous it was to have her mother serving overseas.

"I went to sleep each night with your photo beside me." Penny had to look away then. Away from the almost-shy expression on her daughter's face. Away from the innocent way Gabby gazed up at her, not knowing that her mother was lucky to be coming home when so many of her fellow soldiers hadn't been so fortunate. "There wasn't a day I didn't think about you, honey. I am *so* glad to be home."

Gabby wrapped her arms tight around her again. "Me, too."

Seeing the happy, smug look on her daughter's face made her heart beat so fast she thought it might actually explode from her chest. Having Gabby in her arms made the hours of flying worth it, even if she was only back for a week.

"Hi, Penny."

Penny kept her arms folded around Gabby. Took a deep breath. Then slowly released her daughter, dropped a kiss to her head and straightened.

"Daniel."

This was the only part of the homecoming she hadn't been looking forward to.

She didn't want to let go of Gabby, didn't want this little bubble of happiness to burst. But Daniel's deep voice drew her to her feet.

Penny made herself look up, forced her eyes to lock on his.

On her husband.

He hadn't changed a bit. His hair was thick and rumpled; a hint of stubble grazed his chin, dimple peeking out from the corner of his right cheek.

"It's great to have you home, Penny."

She smiled. Reminded herself that she was here for Gabby. For their daughter.

It was all about Gabby.

She had to be strong.

"It's so good to be back," she replied, looking at her daughter, conscious that her little ears were listening to every word they said. That she didn't know anything was wrong. "I've missed you so much."

Gabby grinned up at her, twirling away to sidle up to her father. She wrapped one arm around his leg, curling into him.

Penny ran her hands down her jeans, the denim rough and foreign beneath her fingertips. After so long in army issue clothing, everything about her jeans and T-shirt seemed…unusual.

Just like standing here with Daniel was unusual.

"Aren't you going to hug her, Daddy?"

Gabby's innocent question made Penny's head spin. Of course she expected to see her parents embrace, to be happy to see one another.

"Ah." What was she meant to say?

"Of course," Daniel said, without a hint of hesitation. "We've missed you so much."

Daniel took a step forward, looked awkward. Penny could feel Gabby watching.

She'd missed him so much, too.

Daniel folded her gently into his arms, his cheek skimming hers as he pressed a barely there kiss against her skin. Penny forced herself to respond, to put her arms around him, too, but it was hard. She so wanted to fall against him, tuck so tight into him that she could hardly breathe, and for everything to be like it always had.

The thought made her pull back and move away, to put distance between them.

Penny glanced at Gabby, to see her smiling again.

"Shall we go home?" Daniel asked.

Penny snapped out of her trance.

"Sure, let's go."

Daniel reached for her bag but she stopped him. Gave him a sharp glare that made his hand pause, midair. Just because she'd hugged him for Gabby's benefit didn't mean she was going to let him off the hook. Was going to pretend like nothing had happened. And she was more than capable of carrying her own bag.

"I'll get it."

She reached for the duffel, careful not to let her hand brush against Daniel's. The pain that crossed his gaze, the way he looked at her, made the dull thud of raw hurt propel through her body again, but she forced it away.

She didn't want to touch him again. It hurt too much.

"Let's go," she said, bag slung over her shoulder.

Gabby reached for her hand, her warm little palm fitting snugly against Penny's.

"Daddy?"

Penny looked over her shoulder as Daniel quickened his pace, taking the other hand that Gabby held outstretched.

Their daughter giggled and laughed, pausing

until she was a step behind them so they could swing her through the air.

"Whee!" she squealed, laughing.

Penny looked over at Daniel, almost smiled to him at Gabby's excitement, then stopped herself.

This was the sort of thing they'd always done, the kind of family they *used* to be.

But she wasn't sure how long they'd be able to pretend they were still the happy family of old.

Because Daniel had ripped her heart out, and she doubted she'd ever be able to forgive him.

"How long are you home for, Mommy?"

She smiled bravely down at her little girl as she swung through the air.

"Not long enough, honey. Not long enough."

Daniel Cartwright was pleased Penny was walking ahead of him.

Because he couldn't take his eyes off her.

The curve of her back and the sway of her body as she moved; the gentleness of her expression, the twist of her smile when she looked at Gabby; the strength of her shoulders as she kept them straight no matter whether she was standing still or walking. The way her long, dark hair fell over her shoulders in a silky curtain.

He'd missed everything about her.

Only he'd always imagined this day to be different. Had seen his wife with her legs wrapped around his waist, lips pressed to his in happiness. The way it had been the last time. When they'd both finished their tours.

If he hadn't stuffed up, that's exactly the homecoming they'd have experienced this time.

"Where's the car?"

Penny's voice took him by surprise. He caught up to them again, having lagged behind to sort out the parking charge.

"Just over there." He pointed ahead.

He tried to catch Penny's eye, to smile at her, to try to connect with her again, but her gaze skipped past him like it was too scared to stop.

"Mommy, are you back forever yet?"

Daniel's heart thudded to his boots.

"Sweetheart, we've already had this conversation," he told her.

This time Penny did look at him, like she didn't want to have to answer their daughter alone. Or maybe like she didn't want to answer at all.

Daniel took the lead.

"Remember how I told you?" he asked Gabby, crouching down before her, holding her hand. "Mommy is here for your birthday, for the *whole week,* but she has to go back."

"To where?"

Daniel heard Penny sigh, like this was a conversation she wasn't ready to have. Yet.

"To work," she said, before crouching down beside him.

Daniel fought not to close his eyes. It was too close. Her body so near to his that he missed her like a fish deprived of water. Even after all this time, he knew how soft her skin would feel against his, the way her body would mold against his.

"Why?" Gabby's lower lip had started to tremble.

"I promise I'll only go away one more time," Penny told her, stroking her hair. "You'll only have to see me go away once more, and then I'll be home with you forever. I promise. I won't leave you again."

Daniel glanced at her, met Penny's eyes, before she looked away.

They'd said that before. That it was the last time. Only Penny hadn't had a choice about her involuntary extension of service.

"Mommy has a really important job," Daniel explained, shuffling closer to Gabby. "Do you remember how I told you that Mommy works for all of America? That she helps to keep everyone safe, with lots of other brave men and women."

Gabby nodded, but her eyes were full to overflowing with tears.

Penny gave him a sharp stare, like they would be talking about this later, but he didn't stop. Gabby didn't know exactly what Penny did, but he hadn't been able to dodge her questions forever. He'd had to tell her *something*. Skirting around the fact she was a soldier wasn't always that easy.

"So when your mommy is away, we have to be brave, because even though we miss her she's a very important woman. Lots of other people need her, too."

Gabby threw her arms around him, tucked her little face into his shoulder and started to sob.

Penny looked as though her heart was broken in two, like she was shattering into a million tiny pieces inside. She swayed back on her haunches before rising, pressed her palms to her cheeks.

Daniel would have said sorry. Felt guilty that he held Gabby when Penny was clearly so desperate to touch, to hold, their daughter.

But there were only so many times he could say sorry. And the next time he said it, he wasn't going to stop until Penny was convinced he meant it.

The short car journey home passed mercifully quickly, Penny content to sit in the backseat alongside Gabby and listen to her chatter away about her life. Daniel sat alone in the front, focused on the road, but that didn't stop him from casting the occasional glance in the rearview mirror at the tender and somehow blissfully normal scene taking place in the rear of the car.

Penny helped Gabby out of the car and let Daniel get her bag this time. She kept hold of her hand, listening to her babble, pleased she was so happily unaware of the tension in the air. As soon as they were through the front door, Grabby dropped her hand and shot ahead down the hall.

It was a strange feeling, coming home. After so

long away and so long imagining what it would be like to be back, it was strangely foreign. It was her home and yet it wasn't all at the same time.

"It is great to have you home, Penny."

She turned at Daniel's words.

"I'm pleased I came back."

He looked hurt, but she wasn't going to feel bad.

"Gabby was so excited when she found out you were coming to her party."

Penny walked to the kitchen bench, spying a cake box. She lifted the lid and smiled when she saw what sat beneath.

"Dora the Explorer, huh?"

Daniel stepped closer. She fought not to move back. Stood her ground.

"It's her favorite," he said, voice low.

Penny hated that she didn't know these kinds of things. What her daughter loved most right now, the things that they didn't talk about over the phone. The things she'd missed out on. Her favorite television shows, dolls, that sort of thing.

She'd never imagined herself as an absentee mother. Had always wanted to be hands-on and at home, and she still did.

"The cake's beautiful," Penny said.

And it was. Pink and purple swirls of icing surrounded the center figure—every little girl's dream.

"It's exactly the kind of cake I would have chosen for her, Daniel."

They stood, not saying anything. Penny's eyes were still trained on the cake. She didn't want to look anywhere else. Was too afraid to look elsewhere.

"Penny, do you want me to move out while you're here?"

Daniel took her by surprise. Move out? She hadn't even thought beyond arriving home, let alone how they'd manage to spend the coming days together.

"Maybe," she said, unsure.

"I've made arrangements to crash at Tom's place, if you want me to." He paused. "I'll understand, you just say the word."

Penny watched as he swallowed, could see the movement of his throat, like he was nervous. Like he was hoping she would say no. Or maybe he was hoping she'd say yes so he didn't have to be under the same roof as her.

"Maybe that would be best," she said, forcing herself to stay calm. Not to get angry.

Although then they'd have to explain to Gabby. Figure out what to say to her, how to tell her.

"Sure," he replied, voice strained. "It's not a problem."

*Argh.* It was so difficult. The entire thing was just so messy.

Daniel nodded. Looked somehow like the wind had been blown from his sails.

She wanted to stare at him, then shake him. Slap him. Yell at him. She had so much pent-up anger that she needed to release, but it was all trapped within her. And she wasn't going to let it go, not when Gabby was within hearing distance.

"I'll hang around for a bit, then head off."

She gave him a half smile. While they were under the same roof, around their daughter, what she wanted was to be civil. To maintain her dignity.

"Coffee?"

Penny nodded and walked over to the pantry. She opened it and looked at the party supplies. He'd made a big effort.

"So you're all set for Saturday?"

He chuckled. "Yeah, as set as you can be for a fifth birthday party."

"Anything I can do to help?"

Daniel caught her eye when she looked over at him. She didn't look away. Something within her stirred, if only for a moment.

Something deep inside flickered when his pupils locked on hers.

She swallowed, hard, then focused on the window instead. Forced herself to.

Because she didn't have to wonder what that something was.

It was love.

No matter how much he'd hurt her, no matter how much pain hammered at her heart, she still loved Daniel.

And she probably always would.

"Penny, I…"

She shook her head. "No, Daniel. Let's not, okay?"

He squared his shoulders. "Penny, please…"

"Mom!"

She dragged her eyes away from Daniel as Gabby called out. She wasn't ready to have that particular conversation. Not yet.

Daniel sighed. She saw it and heard it, but ignored it.

"Coming, honey."

Penny didn't look back at him.

This trip home was about her daughter. There was no room for nostalgia, for thinking about what could have been. She was home for Gabby's birthday, and in less than seven days she'd be getting back on a plane, not coming back until her tour was over for good.

Until then, it was all about Gabby.

No matter how much she ached inside.

Daniel watched Penny move down the hall. He ignored the burning pain in his fingertips as the steaming-hot mug stung his skin. It only made him grip the ceramic handle tighter.

*I'm sorry.* That's what he'd wanted to say. *I'm so damn sorry and I don't know how I'll ever prove it to you.*

He'd told her over the phone, but he had wanted to look her in the eye and tell her to her face. Even if it didn't make a difference, it was something he wanted to say. Needed to say. To convince her that he meant it, that it wasn't just something he felt he should say.

Instead he watched her walk down the hall toward their daughter's room. His wife. Powerless to stop her, no matter how much he wanted to beg for her forgiveness.

"Daddy!"

Gabby was hollering down the hall at him now.

"Yeah?" he called back.

"Come over here!"

Daniel put down the mug after taking a sip and followed in Penny's footsteps.

They were sitting on the bed when he walked in, Gabby cross-legged with toys around her and Penny perched on the edge, a doll in one hand.

Penny looked up at him, gave him *that* look again, and he stared straight back at her. Would have done anything to have looked into her eyes all day, whispered to her and promised to do better, convinced her how much he loved her.

But he couldn't say anything, and he knew she didn't want to hear it anyway. Not right now.

"You showing Mom your things?"

Gabby nodded, her eyes bright. "She didn't even know about my new favorite toys."

Daniel moved slowly across the room and sat on the far edge of the bed. "That's why you have to tell Mommy about all the things you do when she's away. Every time she calls you."

Gabby shook her head. "But she's home now." In complete denial.

Daniel cringed. If only she were. Home for good, that was. It didn't seem to matter how many times he told Gabby, she was holding on to her mother being back forever.

"Remember we talked about this, hon," he told her. "Mom is only back for a week."

Gabby looked down, fingering the doll on her lap.

"Do you want to play with me?" she asked, shyly watching her mother.

Daniel turned away as Penny shuffled across the bed on her knees to sit beside their daughter.

"I'd love to."

He stood up and walked from the room as Penny spoke, not wanting to see the tears in Penny's eyes as she snuggled up beside Gabby.

Because he would have done anything to snuggle right up beside his two girls.

Instead he was heading back down the hall to

confirm his accommodation arrangement for the night. Preparing to be alone, instead of with his family.

Daniel squared his shoulders and went outside, needing the fresh air.

He had been such an idiot. A fool.

If he could turn back time, change the decision he'd made, he would do it in a heartbeat.

But there was no changing the past.

Even if it did seem like a long shot, no matter how strained things might be between them, he still believed.

In the power of love. In the strength of their marriage.

He dug his heel into the top of his other foot. Stomped down hard, trying to fight the hot rush of tears as they pressed down hard, burning at the backs of his eyes.

Daniel wiped hard at his face, knuckles into his eyes.

He wasn't the kind of guy who cried, couldn't remember the last time he'd felt the sting of tears pierce his eyeballs.

He only had six and a half days to make Penny

fall in love with him again, and he was going to make the most of every single minute.

Because he loved his wife and he wasn't going to walk away without a fight.

# CHAPTER TWO

PENNY made her way back down the hall. She didn't know whether to be smiling or frowning. Laughing or crying.

Part of her was so overwhelmingly happy about being home, yet it was heartbreaking at the same time. She'd never resented her four years of service, not when the army had given her so much, but being here with Gabby made her realize how much she was missing out on. How much she just wanted to be a mommy.

She saw Daniel sitting on the sofa, feet up on the coffee table as he watched a game of football, volume down low.

"Hey," she said, letting him know she was standing behind him.

He flicked the television off and swung his feet down.

"Where's Gabby?"

Penny moved slowly around the edge of the

sofa and sat down in the chair opposite. She stifled a laugh. Getting Daniel to turn a game off wasn't usually so simple as her walking into the room.

"She fell asleep while I was reading a story to her. I hope that's okay?"

She had no idea if she even napped during the day still or not.

Daniel smiled. "Yeah, that's fine. She wouldn't go to bed until late last night because she was so excited about you coming home, and she was up at the crack of dawn this morning."

"Me, too," Penny said, yawning. "It's been a long twenty-four hours."

Daniel nodded, leaning back, like he was starting to relax.

"I still remember my last trip home. It seemed to take forever, but it's worth it in the end, right?"

They stared at one another, so much unsaid. So much to say.

But right now it was easier to skirt around certain conversations.

"Do you miss it?"

She'd been wondering for so long.

"Yeah," he said, and she could see the honesty

shining through his eyes. "Yeah, I miss it, but I think being home's worth the sacrifice."

She bet it was. If she'd had the choice, she'd be home, too. Had thought she would have been.

"I love what I do, Daniel, but this whole stop-loss thing seems so unfair." Penny rubbed at her temple, tired from thinking about the whole thing. "I'll never forget that the army paid for my last three years of college, but I've done my time."

"I know."

She sighed and tried to relax. There was no point going over and over it again. They were entitled to extend her enlistment contract to retain her, end of story. Once this tour was over, she'd be home free, so she had to tough it out.

"Let's forget my problem," she said, pleased to change the topic. "How's your job going?"

Daniel shrugged. "It's fine, but it's not the same."

Penny leaned forward slightly, waiting to hear, *wanting* to hear what he had to say. Because even though their marriage was in tatters, and being near him, touching him, hurt, she still cared.

"I'm doing contract work for the navy still, and

it cuts me up sometimes to see the boys going off for work. Seeing them all together, doing their thing, watching the other naval aviators heading out is tough."

"While you're stuck on the ground working on the choppers," she finished for him.

"Yeah," he said. "While I'm tinkering with them to get them running properly, and they're out in the Seahawks."

She didn't miss the almost bitter edge to his voice.

They sat in silence, not looking at one another, yet not ready to stop talking either. To get up and walk away.

"Not that I'm complaining," he quickly corrected himself. "It's just, I don't know, different."

"It's what we always planned, though, right?" she asked, knowing they were both thinking it.

Him in the navy serving out his eight-year term, her finishing her degree through the army scholarship program then serving for four years. Only she'd never expected to be deployed overseas, let alone retained beyond her specified term.

"Me as a helicopter mechanic and you as a physio with your own practice. The house with the big backyard, maybe even another little one on the way."

His words seeped through her body. It was the picture-perfect description she'd always imagined. What they'd always talked about.

Penny looked down, couldn't meet his gaze any longer. Up until a couple of months ago, she'd thought that was still what would be happening. Even if it was going to be a year or so later than they'd expected.

"Penny…"

She held up her hand, strength back, rippling in waves through her body. "Don't, Daniel. Please, just don't." Penny knew what he was going to say. What he was going to bring up.

"I owe it to you, Penny," he said, voice low now. Like he was in pain. *"Please."*

"You owed it to me to be faithful." She hurled the words at him, her calmness replaced by hurt. Unable to hold it in check. Thinking of what he'd done to her and wishing upon wishing that it hadn't happened. That everything was back to normal again. *But it wasn't.* "And I *do not* want to be having this conversation right now."

He shut his eyes. She watched him do it, wanted

to do the same, but was holding so tightly on to her strength that she didn't dare let herself.

When he opened them again and looked at her, she saw a sadness, a deepness there that she'd never seen before on his face. A hurt that she felt mirrored in her own steely gaze.

"Penny, I love you so much," he said, leaning forward, hands on his knees. "I know you don't believe me, but I'm so sorry for what I did. If there was anything I could do to make it up to you, any way to prove to you that it meant nothing to me, that it was the worst decision I've ever made in my life, I'd do it."

Penny stood then, moved past him. Brushed fiercely past his outstretched hand, not wanting to touch him. Not having the strength to be so close to him.

Because goddamn it, *it hurt*.

"Trust was all we had, Daniel, and you broke that."

She couldn't face him because tears were streaming down her cheeks, leaving wet, slippery marks across her skin. As they curled toward her mouth she let her tongue flick out to catch the salty wetness of them.

Had serving her country, being away for so long, caused her marriage to fail? Was it *her* fault? Did she have to shoulder some of the blame?

"It wasn't all we had, Penny," he said softly.

Anger built within her, compelled her tears to stop. "It was everything, Daniel. Because without it, we have nothing."

He stood then, reached for her wrist. She yanked it back, not letting his skin connect with hers.

"We have Gabby."

She nodded. "She will always be the most important person in my life, Daniel. And I know you're a great dad. Nothing changes that."

He stared at her. Waiting for the *but*.

Penny kept it inside her mouth, though, not letting the words spill.

*But you're a crappy husband,* she wanted to say. *And you've hurt me more than I ever thought was possible.* No matter how hard this was for him, no matter what he'd been through, he was here and she was going back to no-man's-land.

"I'm sorry, Penny. I don't know how else to say

it to you, or what I can do. But I'm sorry and I love you."

She swallowed, shaking her head to stop the words from settling in her mind.

"I'm sorry, too, Daniel," she replied, squaring her shoulders and looking him straight in the eye. Penny took a deep, shaky breath. "And for the record, it's not because I'm incapable of forgiving, it's because I can't forget, Daniel. I don't know if I'll *ever* be able to forget what you did."

Couldn't forget that he'd been with another woman. That his hands had touched another's skin, his mouth had traced another's lips.

It made her skin crawl.

This time it was him who was swallowing, who was shaking his head sadly.

"I don't know what else I can say to prove to you how important you are to me. How much I love you."

She shook her head. "Can we drop it, Daniel, please? I just want us to play happy families for Gabby's birthday, remain civil and be the parents I know we both want to be."

"Daddy?"

Gabby's little voice rang out down the hall, still croaky with sleep.

Daniel went to move, but Penny stepped in front of him. "Let me."

He didn't resist.

"I don't want to have this conversation while Gabby's around. I'm only here for the week, and there's no point in upsetting her."

Daniel stood, arms hanging loosely by his side, posture alert, tall, not yet defeated. So unlike the strong man she was used to, the one who would never back down.

Like he had so much left to say, like he wanted to fight for what he wanted, but was unsure how the hell to do it.

"It's your call, Penny."

She turned her back on him and went to her daughter.

Tears still threatened, but she shrugged them away. After what she'd survived in the army, what she'd seen and experienced, she should have been able to cope with this. But nothing she'd seen serving overseas could compare.

Her heart was breaking, slowly, over and over, and there was nothing she could do about it.

No way to help it heal before it shattered all over again. Like a record stuck on repeat.

To a very bad song.

"I—want—Daddy!"

Daniel entered the room to see Penny's face crumpled. She composed herself within a half second, but he didn't miss it.

And he didn't want to cut her out, either.

"Honey, why don't you let Mommy help you?"

She shook her head, determination clear on her face. Burning in her eyes.

"No! I—want—you!" She punched out each word.

Geez. The last thing they needed right now, with everything this tense, was Gabby having a tantrum. She'd been so good lately, had hardly planted her bottom lip down in anger and refused to do what he asked for months.

Until now.

Her timing was impeccable.

"I'll go and get dinner started." The sadness in Penny's voice made him look up.

He shook his head, resisting the urge to glare at Gabby.

"No, stay," he asked.

Penny looked up at him, hope shining in her eyes.

"Can Mommy help us?"

Gabby caught her bottom lip between her teeth, chewing on it softly. She nodded, eyes flickering between them.

"Okay, then," he said.

Penny shot him a grateful look. He fought to break his gaze, to pull his eyes from hers. After so many years of being so close, of knowing what the other was thinking before they said something; of touching each other, brushing against one another without even thinking about it.

And now the distance was painful.

Daniel walked over to the closet and looked through Gabby's clothes. "Pink T-shirt?"

He looked back over his shoulder as Gabby sat on the bed, still pouting. "The sparkly one."

Daniel laughed, catching Penny's raised eyebrow as he did so.

"Come over here," he said to her, beckoning with one finger.

Penny pushed off from the doorjamb where

she'd been leaning. She looked unsure, but she did it anyway.

"Check out the sparkly T-shirts and tops," he said, voice low, although he knew Gabby could hear him. "And she orders me to get the sparkly one like I'd know which one she means."

Penny laughed, but she reached for a soft, pink tee with a dog on the front. He watched as she fingered it, pleased that the air between them had relaxed, if only temporarily.

"I remember buying this," Penny said, lifting the top and pressing it to her face. Inhaling the scent. "We saw it after lunch, on our way back, before I shipped out. It was too big for her then."

Penny was right. It was the day before he'd waved her goodbye. The day before he'd effectively become a solo dad. Been left alone.

He pushed the thoughts away. She was here now and that's what mattered.

"Is this the one?" Penny asked, voice filled with hope as she held it out.

Gabby nodded.

Daniel doubted it was the one she'd originally had in mind, but he was grateful she'd agreed. For Penny's sake.

"Pants?" he called over his shoulder.

"Skirt!" she responded.

He glanced at Penny as she chuckled.

"Is she always like this?" she whispered.

Daniel moved his head slowly from side to side, pleased to have an excuse to bend closer to her. To reduce the physical void between them.

"When you left, I used to joke with my Mom that she was a mini-tyrant. At least once a week. But she hasn't been like this in ages."

Penny looked sad. "Has my coming home upset her? Should I have just stayed away until I could come back for good?"

Daniel couldn't resist touching her then, had to connect with her.

*Because she was wrong.*

"Penny, you coming home is the best thing that's happened to us. Don't go beating yourself up over one temper tantrum thrown by an over-tired child."

She gave him a weak smile.

"But she only seems to want you. It's like I've been made redundant."

He closed his hand around her shoulder, keeping his touch light when what he really wanted to do was draw her against him and hold her close. To comfort her.

"I'm what she's been used to this past year," he said, looking into her eyes. "Once you're home for good she'll probably forget all about me within a week."

"I doubt it," Penny said.

But the flicker in her eyes told him that she hoped it was at least partly true. She angled her body slightly, as if asking him to remove his hand, but not wanting to shrug it away.

Or maybe she just didn't want Gabby to see her do it.

Either way, whatever her reasons, he had no intention of making her feel uncomfortable.

But when he took his hand away, his skin was left feeling cold. And he wished he'd had permission to keep it there longer, all night if she'd let him.

"Shall I go and check on dinner? Your family will be here soon."

Daniel didn't answer, moved himself away instead, not wanting to crowd her. He turned to Gabby.

"Can Mommy help do your hair while I go do dinner?"

Gabby went to shake her head, but he stared at her, gave her a look that he hoped said that it was time to behave. He could see the defiance gone from her face, the determination of before as good as disappeared.

Gabby sighed, dramatically, more teenager than kid. "Okay."

Daniel was sure Penny's heart had broken all over again, but he left them to it. No one had ever said this would be easy, but they all had to figure it out. Had to cope.

Somehow.

And right now he had to prepare for seeing his mother and his brother. They might be his family, but they were treating him like the black sheep after what he'd done.

As if he wasn't beating himself up enough without having them glare at him, too. Without acting like they'd never speak to him again, if it wasn't for Gabby, because of what he'd done.

Daniel dropped a kiss to Gabby's head as he passed and resisted the urge to look at Penny again.

Instead he walked out the door and into the kitchen, and poured himself a glass of wine.

Tonight was going to be a long night.

This was harder than Penny had expected. When she'd been away, she'd imagined that the day she returned home would be the day everything returned to normal.

Daniel had put an end to that with his infidelity, but she hadn't expected it to be so difficult with Gabby.

She heard a knock at the door as she was pressing gloss to her lips. She was nervous, which was stupid, given that Daniel's family had been her family, too, since before she'd joined the army. But still. If their marriage was truly over, would they still consider her family? Still want to see her? Still feel the same about her?

Prickles tingled across her skin at the thought of losing them, too. Daniel's mother was like her own. A surrogate for the one she'd lost. And his brother? She'd always been so close to him, but surely brothers' blood ran too thick for her to expect him to remain close to her.

"Mommy!"

Penny looked up at her reflection, pausing to consider herself in the mirror before she braved their guests. There were tiny lines playing across the skin at the corners of her eyes that hadn't been there when she'd been deployed for the second time, a tiredness that had crept up on her without her realizing. And there was a sadness, a hollowness in her expression that she had felt but not seen before, and that scared her.

Because until now, she'd worried about smile lines around her mouth, not frown wrinkles.

Penny sighed and smoothed the soft fabric of her top down her torso. She glanced down at her hand and looked at how tanned it was. But there was no white line where her wedding ring had once sat, and the hollow at the front of her neck was bare. She'd always kept her wedding rings on a chain there, the weight of them reminding her of home, but she'd removed them the day Daniel had told her what he'd done, and she'd never put them on again.

If he hadn't told his family before, they were going to figure it out pretty quick. His mother would notice her bare hand the moment she saw it.

"Mommy!" Gabby hollered again.

"Coming," she called back.

She didn't see Gabby when she emerged into the living room, but she did see Tom walking through the front door.

And a laugh caught in her throat. A laugh that could so easily have turned into a sob.

Maybe he did think of her like his sister, if his body language was anything to go by.

Daniel stepped forward to shake his hand, or maybe to pull him in for the hug-and-back-slap thing they used to do. But the look on Tom's face spelled anger. The same look she bet he wore when things weren't going his way on a mission. She might be a soldier, but even she knew how tough and determined a Navy SEAL could be!

Tom glared at Daniel, pausing only to smack him on the side of the head with his open palm as he passed.

"Ow!"

Daniel reached to where he'd been knocked, hand over his left ear.

"Idiot," Tom muttered.

Daniel didn't look amused, but he didn't argue either.

Penny took a deep, gulping breath before stepping fully into the room. At least they knew. It would have been harder if Daniel hadn't been truthful about what had happened between them. About what he'd done.

She cleared her throat, announcing her presence.

"Penny!"

His mother's excited call made Penny forget her thoughts. Made her worries drain away.

"Oh, Pen, it's so good to have you home safe and sound."

She let herself be folded into the warm, welcoming embrace of the woman who'd been like her mother for the past eight years.

"Thanks for coming over, Vicki," Penny mumbled against her mother-in-law's shoulder, holding her back, tight.

She found herself being held at arm's length to be inspected.

"Thanks?" Vicki repeated, shaking her head. "The last thing I need is thanks! I've missed you every day that you've been away. Daniel couldn't have kept me away if he tried."

"Me neither."

Penny turned to see Tom behind her, arms held out. She stepped into them, returning the bear hug he offered.

"Hey," she said, relaxing against him.

"You look good, little miss sergeant," he said with a laugh. "Ready to give up being G.I. Jane yet?"

"You ready for a wife?" she quipped.

She watched as he shot Daniel a look from across the room and then focused soft eyes on her. Eyes that spelled sadness and compassion in one gentle look. "You've set the bar too high. How could I find anyone as good as you?"

Tension seemed to swirl through the room. Penny wished it away.

"Champagne," Vicki announced. "Let's open a bottle and celebrate."

Gabby appeared, sidling up against her grandmother.

"What are we celebrating?" she asked.

Penny loved her innocence.

"Your mother arriving home, of course!" Vicki told her, bending to kiss Gabby's cheek.

Daniel walked over, glaring back at his brother

now, as if telling him he wouldn't be so easily intimidated, not in front of his daughter.

"We're celebrating the best birthday present ever, Gabby," Daniel said softly, gaze unwaveringly focused on Penny.

She felt as if it were only the two of them in the room. As if everyone else had disappeared and they were all that was left, alone, the pair of them.

Sweat seemed to clam against her skin, making her flushed and nervous at the same time.

"Your mother coming home is the best gift we could ever have asked for."

Gabby giggled. The sound, combined with her tiny hands linking around Penny's leg, burst the bubble Penny had lost herself in. Made her look away from Daniel.

"That *and* a bike, though, right?" she asked.

All the adults in the room laughed, Penny included. A real laugh that came from deep within her belly.

"You'll just have to wait and see, miss," Daniel told her.

Gabby tugged Penny forward, resting her head against her thigh.

"I've been a really good girl, you know," she said, eyes wide as she watched her mom.

Penny looked up at Daniel and couldn't help but smile. Gabby's tantrum earlier forgotten as if it had never happened. Even though it broke her heart not to be touching him, to be missing out on the casual contact they'd always enjoyed.

Because this child, the daughter they'd made together, was like the glue holding the tender pieces of their life together.

She was the most precious gift in the world. One they'd always share, no matter what.

And she was precisely the reason Penny wished she could forget what Daniel had done and make everything go back to normal.

But she couldn't forget, and Daniel couldn't take back what he'd done.

Which meant that Penny had no idea what the hell they were going to do with the mess they'd made of their lives.

And their marriage.

"Champagne, Penny?"

She held her hand out, forcing a smile as Vicki produced a full glass for her.

"And one for the little lady," Vicki announced, passing Gabby a glass of something fizzy.

Penny leaned into her mother-in-law's embrace and held back tears.

This was what she'd missed. Being part of a family. Being loved.

Because Daniel's infidelity had made her feel so unloved she could hardly catch her breath.

Once, she'd lost her mother, her only family, and wondered how she could survive it. But then Daniel's family had made her feel like one of their own. Without them, it would be like losing her mother all over again.

# CHAPTER THREE

PENNY sat at the table with her mother-in-law. She let her elbows rest on it and slumped forward slightly. Finally able to relax.

Gabby was in bed, the boys were in the kitchen doing the dishes, and it was just her and Vicki.

She looked up as Vicki gave her a small smile.

"Is it weird that I want to say sorry to you?" she asked Vicki.

The older woman nodded, scooting over in the chair closer to Penny.

"It's weird because it's wrong," Vicki said firmly. "You have nothing to apologize for and I have everything to be sorry for."

Penny pursed her lips, but she didn't say anything. Couldn't. Because for once in her life she didn't know what the hell to say. She was sorry that her marriage to Vicki's son was over, even though it wasn't technically her fault.

Or maybe she did know what to say.

It was simply that the words were struggling to form in her throat.

"Did Daniel…" She paused, glancing over her shoulder to make sure the guys were still in the kitchen. "Did he tell you why? I mean, did he tell you what he did?"

Vicki nodded sadly, reaching a shaking hand for her wineglass and taking a long, slow sip.

"I'm so sorry, Penny. I can't believe that after what his father put me through, that he's turned around and done the same thing to you."

Penny didn't know what to say. Had Daniel really turned into his father? She doubted it. He'd made a serious mistake, but she'd never lump him into the same category as his cheating, lying father.

"At least he told me," Penny whispered, scared of her own voice. Of her own thoughts. "That counts for something, right?"

Vicki reached for her hand and squeezed it. "It might count, but it doesn't excuse what he did. All I can say is sorry, and I hope you know that I'm here for you. No matter what you decide."

She looked up.

A tremor ran through her. Did Vicki not know

that she'd told Daniel it was over? Did she expect her to take him back?

"Vicki, I—I can't just forgive him." The words were flat, almost impossible to say. "It's not that simple."

"I know more than anyone how hard your decision is, all I'm asking is that you hear him out. Take your time in making a decision that will last the rest of your life."

Penny sucked back a big, shaky breath.

"Every time I shut my eyes, I see his betrayal. I can picture him with another woman. I want to know every detail and yet I know I'm not strong enough to ask." She shuddered at the thought. "But I love him so much, even though I hate him, too, and I don't know how to make sense of that."

Vicki wiped tears from her own eyes as she reached for Penny again.

"Then that's exactly what you need to tell him, Penny."

"I can't." She choked out her refusal.

"Yes, you can," Vicki insisted. "You owe it to yourself, to the years you've put into this relationship and this marriage, to find out whether you can forgive him."

Penny shook her head. "Even if I can forgive, how do I ever forget? Cheating is a deal breaker for me, Vicki, it always has been."

Her mother-in-law met her gaze. "It's easy to say it's a deal breaker, Penny, before you're actually faced with it happening to you, but this is real. It's happened now, and I'd hate for you to look back in years to come and wish you'd given him a chance to prove himself."

She was his mother. Penny knew that she'd want them to work through this, but still. Was she right? Did she need to pull her head out of the sand it was buried in, be a big girl and give him a chance to prove how sorry he was?

"I've been there, done that." The look on Vicki's face was pained, like it hurt to talk about what she'd gone through. "I'm happy my marriage ended, that I walked away from him and never looked back, because he hurt me *over and over* again." She paused. "If that's how you feel, too, then so be it. All I'm saying is that I want you to be *sure* it's the right decision for *you*."

"I can't just roll over and pretend like nothing happened, Vicki. And I can't do it for Gabby, either. She'll still be a happy, loved child even if our marriage does end." Penny wasn't angry with her for questioning, for bringing it up, because it was a conversation she'd had in her own head over and over, and she didn't have a mother of her own to talk it through with.

"Does that mean you'll give him a chance, though?" Vicki's voice was barely more than a whisper.

Penny half shrugged, her shoulders only just rising before falling back into a slump.

"I don't know."

She honestly didn't. Most of her thought there was no way in hell she could ever forgive him, but some small niggle, something deep within her, wanted to listen to her mother-in-law.

Because maybe she needed to hear him out. Needed to at least try to understand why he'd done it.

Vicki stood, collecting both their glasses from the table as the boys' voices became louder, closer.

"Will you at least think about it?"

She stood, too, hands palms-down on the tabletop.

"I'll think about it, but I'm not making any promises."

Vicki gave her a tight smile. "That's all I'm asking you to do, Pen. I don't want to lose you from this family, you mean too much to me."

Penny sighed.

She didn't want to lose them either. But at the same time, she didn't know whether she had the strength to fight for her marriage, to do what had to be done to resolve their problems.

Because if she forgave Daniel, did that mean she was saying that what he'd done was okay? That it was acceptable? How could she ever trust him again?

Was that the kind of example she wanted to set for her daughter? When she grew up, did she want Gabby to know that she'd taken her father back, even though he'd been unfaithful? It wasn't just about her own feelings; she wanted to be setting the right example for her daughter. She owed it to her to be the best role model she could, to show by example how important it was to have a husband who respected and loved you more than anything in the world.

But at the same time, she loved Daniel more

than heaven and earth combined. Or at least she had. And maybe a part of her still did.

Or maybe she loved the Daniel she'd once known. The Daniel she'd left behind.

The Daniel she'd believed would never cheat on her.

Penny sighed and wished the earth would swallow her up.

She'd come home for her daughter's birthday, yet here she was trying to make the biggest decision of her life.

It wasn't fair. None of it was.

And there was no easy way to do what had to be done.

It was forgive and forget.

The problem was she didn't know if she was capable of either.

Tom pulled Penny in for a quick hug before he ducked out the door.

"Have I told you that I think he's an idiot?" he whispered before he passed.

Penny squeezed him back before letting him disappear out into the warm evening air.

"It was great seeing you both," she said honestly.

"Lovely seeing you, too," her mother-in-law replied, touching her shoulder as she passed her in the doorway.

Daniel stood a step behind her. She could feel him there, even before he said good-night to their guests.

He'd said he was going to stay at Tom's place, but she guessed he wasn't ready to go yet.

She wished he would. Just get in his car and leave. But another part of her didn't want him to go anywhere, didn't want to be alone in the house. When it was so long since she'd been without the company of others.

Even if Gabby was asleep down the hall.

"I'll head off soon," said Daniel, as if he'd read her thoughts.

She turned, slowly.

"You don't have to go," she said, not sure if she was telling the truth or not.

He shuffled a step closer, then seemed to think better of it and stopped, bracing himself against the wall. His big frame like a statue, muscled arms crossed over his chest.

"You need some time alone, and I don't want to crowd you." He paused, as if hoping she'd disagree. Tell him he was wrong. "I'll be back first thing in the morning, and we can open presents and do all that sort of thing then."

Penny stared at her feet, watching the way her toes curled into the carpet. It had been a long time since she'd been able to indulge in bare feet like this, snuggling her toes into the floor. She'd fulfilled her time in the army with a genuine smile on her face and a spring in her step, believing in what she was doing and liking that she was serving her country. It wasn't until she came back to her civilian life that she realized how nice little luxuries like carpet were.

"Maybe you should come past early. You know, so Gabby doesn't realize anything is wrong."

Daniel pushed off from the wall and ran a hand through his hair.

She knew that signal. He only ever did that when he was stressed. Or worried.

"Sure, good idea," he mumbled.

Penny waited for a heartbeat then followed him. Was it so wrong to be unsure? And to want to shield their young daughter from a pain that could hurt so bad her heart could shatter? She didn't want to deal with the questions that would arise from telling her the truth. Not yet.

She didn't want Gabby to think she was to blame, or any other emotions that children felt when they learned their parents no longer wanted to be together. That they didn't love one another enough.

Although in this case it wasn't so much that they'd fallen out of love.

Because every vein, every surge of blood, every fiber within her was screaming that she still loved Daniel.

That he was the reason her heart had had cause to beat for the past ten years. That he was the strike of match to light the fire within her.

He looked back, as if he could hear her inner scream, the demons that were ripping her heart and her emotions to shreds.

"Penny, I know this might be way off base, but you're only here for a few days so I can't hold back."

She reached for the armchair beside her, gripping tight until her knuckles were white, drained of blood.

"Can we just leave it a day, Daniel? I know we have to talk, but I need some time to get my head around everything. To think."

Even though all she'd done was think these past few months.

He nodded. Reluctantly.

"A day, then?" he asked. "Let's spend the day together tomorrow, enjoy the party, and tomorrow night we can talk."

Penny swallowed what felt like a dinner plate. Her mouth was dry and raspy, her breathing shallow.

"Okay," she agreed. "You're right, we do need to talk. I just need some space right now."

Daniel stared at her from across the room, his gaze saying what words could never express.

She knew, because she felt the same look, the same emotions, in her own eyes.

He crossed the room with the stealth of a leopard, feet making the softest of sounds on the carpet.

Daniel stopped a breath away from her, pressed one of his palms to her own as it hung by her side and whispered a kiss across her cheek.

She should have moved, but she didn't.

Couldn't.

"I love you." His words were so soft it was as if they were a part of his slow exhale.

She stood stunned. Watched him walk backward, his eyes never leaving hers, until he reached the hall and had to turn.

Penny stood there, waited for him to collect his already packed overnight bag and let her gaze follow him to the door. Daniel turned, hand raised in a half wave, before opening the door and disappearing into the night.

She waited, frozen, until she heard the car's engine rumble, listened to him pull out of the driveway.

*No.*

She was alone.

Penny thrust her hand up, fisted it into her mouth as a choking sob, a wail, threatened to bubble up from her throat.

Then she fell to her knees, her body weaker than a floppy rubber band.

Tears poured down her cheeks, wet her T-shirt. Choked her.

But she couldn't deny them, not any longer.

As silent sobs raked her chest, she forced her mouth shut to close out any noise.

Gabby was asleep down the hall, the house wasn't empty.

There had been nights when she'd stood in the dark, with only her breath in the cold to remind her that she was still alive, when she'd been serving overseas.

But she'd never, ever been so alone in all her life as she was right now.

# CHAPTER FOUR

"IDIOT, moron, loser...do I need to keep going?"

Daniel scowled as his brother. Yeah, he'd mucked up, but he didn't need to be constantly reminded. He was doing a fine job of that all on his own.

"That's enough, Tom." He grimaced at the growl in his tone.

Tom raised an eyebrow. "Enough? Yet here you are, sleeping on my couch, while your *amazing* wife lies in your bed. *Alone.*"

He shut his eyes. Hell, he'd shut Tom out, too, if he could. But he wasn't going to knock on his mom's door in the middle of the night, and he didn't exactly like his chances of convincing any of his married friends to let him in after dark. Not when they'd no doubt be happily asleep beside their own wives.

"Seriously, Daniel. I just don't get it."

Daniel sat up, pushing the blanket off, anger bubbling like a mini-volcano within him.

"It *is* enough, Tom, because there's nothing I can do about it. Okay?"

Tom put his hands on his knees, as if he was bracing himself, or maybe trying to stop himself from punching Daniel in the nose.

"There's always something you can do."

"Like what?" Daniel was open to suggestions. All he seemed to do these days was try to figure out how he could make things right.

"All I know is that you've got this amazing wife, the kind of girl I'd do anything for, and somehow you managed to stuff it up. Big-time."

Daniel fought not to pummel his fist into something. "Don't you think I know that?" he almost yelled. "If I could take it back I would."

They sat in silence. Daniel's head was pounding.

"You've been different, Daniel," his brother said, voice soft now. The accusations gone.

Daniel clamped his jaw tight, so hard he almost ground his teeth together. But he couldn't stay quiet any longer. It was time to talk. If he couldn't open up to his own brother, how would he ever get it off his chest?

"I miss it, Tom. I miss it so bad."

His brother got up, pulled out two beers from the fridge and passed him one.

"You mean Penny?"

He sighed. A big, deep exhale of air that whooshed from his lungs.

"Of course Penny, but the navy, too. I know I should be grateful to be back here for good, but without Penny, it was so hard adjusting. I miss the guys, I miss the adrenaline rush of being up in the Seahawk, of being on a mission. *I miss it so damn bad.*"

Tom stayed silent, swigging quietly on his beer.

"And then I got so damn lonely, felt so sorry for myself, that I ruined everything." He stared at the ceiling, forcing emotion back down his throat, fighting the feeling of his heart burning to death. "I was so alone, it was like I'd lost everything, and I was so utterly selfish that I ruined my life and hers. I just wish she'd let me try to explain what happened, what I was going through."

Tom leaned toward him, the anger gone, replaced by a look Daniel hoped wasn't pity.

"You stuffed up, bro, but you need to do everything you can to make this right. For you. For Penny. For Gabby."

Daniel twirled the cold bottle in his hands. He didn't know what to do, how to go about it.

"Even if you do get her to listen, you made the choice and this is the consequence. You can't lump any of the blame on Penny." Tom's voice was stern but his gaze was kind. "I can't imagine ever leaving the navy behind, it's my life, but she's your *wife,* Dan. It doesn't matter how hard it is for you, she's more important. It's Penny we're talking about."

He was right, he usually was. Only this time, Daniel had no idea what to do to make things right.

A phone rang.

He looked up, expecting it to be Tom's, before realizing it was his.

Daniel reached for it, almost dropping it when he saw the caller identification.

"Who is it?" Tom asked.

Daniel gulped, pausing before he answered. "Home," he replied, his voice hoarse.

Tom raised an eyebrow again.

It was too late for Gabby to be calling him.

And that left only one option.

*Penny.*

He put his beer down and pressed the phone to his ear.

"Daniel?"

Her voice was shaky, fragile. Like she'd been crying.

"Penny, what's wrong? Is Gabby okay?"

He listened to a muffled noise, hoped she *wasn't* crying, then a sigh.

"I think you need to come home."

Daniel eyed his beer, thankful he hadn't consumed it. He'd have been no help to anyone if he'd drowned his sorrows and hadn't been able to drive.

"I'll be there as quick as I can."

"Thank you," she whispered down the line, before hanging up.

Daniel looked at the makeshift bed on the couch, then over at Tom.

"Go," his brother told him.

Daniel didn't need to be told.

He ran a hand down his jeans, pushing out the

crumples, did the same to his hair and grabbed his keys.

"I'll call you tomorrow," he called over his shoulder.

"Don't bother, I'll be at the party."

The party. He'd almost forgotten. The reason Penny was home.

He threw a hand up in a quick wave and slammed the door behind him.

It didn't matter why Penny needed him. Why she'd called.

Because he'd always be there for her. She'd never have to ask him twice.

He'd been an idiot. *Once.*

In all their years together, all the times they'd spent apart, with her in the army and him in the navy, he'd always been faithful. Never even thought of straying.

He'd been a jerk *once,* and he'd regret that for the rest of his life.

But Tom was right. This was his chance to make things right, to make it up to Penny. No matter what it took, no matter what the consequences.

Because the consequences of not saving his

marriage weren't even worth contemplating. Everything else could be overcome, dealt with, but letting Penny slip from his life would be something he'd regret forever.

He loved Penny, and he'd do his darndest to prove it to her.

Starting now.

# CHAPTER FIVE

PENNY slumped against the wall in the hallway. She'd never felt so hopeless, so *useless* before.

And even though she knew it was rude to eavesdrop, would have told her daughter off for doing the same thing, she couldn't help but listen.

"Why did you leave me, Daddy? I was scared."

Penny shut her eyes.

"I didn't leave you, Gabby. Mommy was here and I was only visiting Uncle Tom."

"But it's the middle of the night."

Penny smiled. She might only be five, but it seemed Gabby was too smart to be fooled.

"Sweetheart, I thought you'd enjoy spending some time just with Mommy."

Silence stretched out. Penny wanted to walk away, she did, but her feet were stuck to the spot as if glue had fixed them.

"She didn't tuck me back in the way you do when I woke up."

Penny listened to Daniel chuckle, while her own heart shattered. Was pierced by shards of glass.

"There's no right way to tuck a little girl into bed, miss," he said sternly. "So long as it's followed by a kiss and lots of love."

Silence again.

"Did Mommy kiss you?"

Penny held her breath. She hoped Gabby was nodding. She had kissed her. Had kissed her so many times she had hardly been able to stop herself.

"Then Mommy did tuck you in the right way after all, didn't she?"

"But you weren't there, in your bed, when I climbed in."

This time it was Daniel who sighed.

"Mom is very tired, and I wanted her to have the bed to herself. So she could, ah, spread out and relax."

They hadn't thought this through at all.

Penny made herself move then, propelled herself down the hall rather than torturing herself over listening any longer.

\* \* \*

"Penny?"

She stirred the chocolate in the pot, wooden spoon tracing circles around and around.

"In here," she called softly.

Daniel appeared a moment later.

"Hot chocolate?" he asked.

Penny raised her eyes. "Yeah. Want one?"

He gave her a gentle smile that raised one side of his mouth into the kindest of curves. "I'd love one."

Penny reached for another mug, finished stirring and poured even amounts into each one. She passed Daniel his, then cupped her hands around her own. It was hot, but she didn't mind the light burning sensation.

It took some of the pain away from her mind. Where she kept replaying Gabby's words over and over.

"This isn't going to work, is it?" she asked.

Confusion crossed Daniel's face.

"I mean this whole not-telling-her thing," she corrected. "She's going to figure it out soon, and I think *we* need to figure out what to tell her."

Daniel sipped his chocolate slowly. "What do you want to tell her?"

Penny raised her shoulders before letting them fall again. "Honestly? I don't know, Daniel, but it doesn't feel right pretending."

"So let's not pretend," he said, eyes shining.

What? "You want to tell her?"

He shook his head, eyes burning the deepest of browns, as dark as the rich chocolate she'd stirred in the pot. "No," he said firmly. "I want to prove myself to *you* so we don't have to pretend to *her*. I want another chance, Penny. I want it so bad, but I don't know what to say or do to convince you to say yes. I know we said we'd wait until tomorrow night, but we're here now and I think we need to talk."

She shook her head. *No*.

This was not a conversation she wanted to be having right now. She didn't feel strong enough to go there.

"Penny?"

"Daniel, I…"

He held up a hand, as if he didn't want to hear what she was going to say. Didn't want to give her the chance to say no.

"I know you're angry with me, Pen, and I know

I deserve it. Hell, do I know I deserve it," he told her. "But you're only here for a week, right?"

She nodded, scared of where this was going. "Six days as of right now."

He put his mug down and reached for her, then folded his hands back against his own body, as if he wasn't sure what her reaction would be to his touch.

She was glad he hadn't made contact.

Touching him right now would be too soon. She was still too raw.

"We can pretend for Gabby's sake. And I mean really pretend. But at the same time, I want to give us a go for real."

Penny's head started shaking all on its own.

She was *not* just going to pretend like everything was normal. Not to that extent.

But then, hadn't they been doing exactly that already for Gabby's sake?

"Please, Pen. Let me prove myself to you," he said, his voice quiet yet powerful. Deep and strong. "If you want to walk away from us, from our marriage, by the time you get back on that plane, then I'll file for separation. You can move on and start over."

She gulped. "What's the other option?"

This time Daniel smiled so genuinely that his eyes crinkled in the corners. "We fall in love again and give our marriage a second chance."

Penny stood still, unmoving, in shock.

She couldn't answer him.

Instead she turned sharply and walked down the hall.

Daniel didn't say anything, but her mind was racing. Ideas, realities, *possibilities* powering through her mind.

She reached the end of the hallway, not sure what she was doing, or what she should do.

But one niggling thought in particular wouldn't leave her alone.

What if she did have the ability to forgive? To forget?

What if, by some miracle, Daniel was right? That their marriage did deserve a second shot?

What if she did owe it to him to try to understand?

Right now, she didn't believe it. Couldn't believe that they could ever get past this.

But he was right about fooling Gabby. If they

weren't going to tell her the truth, they needed to make a better effort at pretending.

She took a deep, shuddering breath and marched back down the hall.

Daniel hadn't moved.

"If we're going to do this for real you may as well come to bed," she said, voice shaking, trying so hard to be brave.

Daniel looked up when she turned. His eyes smiled at her. But he didn't say a word.

Instead he followed her silently down the hall.

Goose bumps rippled up and down Penny's shoulders, across her back.

She was more nervous than a virgin on her wedding night. Even though she'd be changing in the bathroom and wearing pajamas to bed.

Even though Daniel had been her husband for almost seven years already and her partner for ten.

Daniel sat on the edge of the bed. It was like being in a stranger's room, it seemed so foreign.

He ran a hand across the quilt, resisting the urge to look over his shoulder. Penny was in the adjoining bathroom, he could hear water running still, and he didn't know what to do.

Whether he should leave her side lamp on and get under the covers, roll over and at least pretend he was asleep. Or sit up with his light on, waiting for her.

Or offer to sleep on the chair. Or the floor.

Daniel sighed. He didn't know what the hell to do. When all he wanted was to do the right thing.

The running water stopped, leaving only deafening silence in its place.

Daniel peeled off his T-shirt, half folded it and dropped it to the floor. He did the same with his jeans, pulling them off, then his socks.

He left his boxers on, slid beneath the covers and rolled onto his side after turning his lamp off.

He listened to Penny as the doorknob turned, listened to her pad softly across the carpet.

Then felt her climb into bed as the weight of her body folded into the mattress.

The void between them seemed enormous. The ocean may as well have separated them. Even with his back turned, he could feel her there and at the same time he couldn't.

Could hear the gentle inhale of her breath, could sense the indent of her body beside his.

But the cold sheets stretched so far between them that he would have had to reach right out to brush his skin against hers.

And he wanted to. *Damn, did he want to.*

Instead he silently pummelled his fist into his pillow and squeezed his eyes shut, hoping sleep would come quickly.

"'Night."

Penny's soft voice jolted his eyes back open.

"Good night," he said back, voice hoarse.

He wondered how long they'd lie there, awake yet pretending they weren't. Both thinking, wondering, waiting.

So close but so far apart.

She'd agreed to pretend. For now.

So maybe, just maybe, she'd give him that second chance he was so desperate for.

# CHAPTER SIX

DANIEL woke up early. He didn't know what woke him, but he knew why he'd slept so well, and why he didn't want to move.

It had been almost a year since he'd woken with the weight of his wife in bed with him, the warmth of her body, the sound of her gentle breathing. It paralyzed him. Made him hold his own breath for fear of waking her. He stayed as still as an arrow stuck in timber, barely quivering.

Somehow in the night they'd gone from being separated by cold sheets to rolling against one another. Bodies skimming, touching enough for him to want to carefully place an arm around Penny and draw her in close.

But he didn't.

Because he hadn't earned the right to touch her yet. To hold her deep in his embrace.

He'd waited for this for so long. *Wanted this for so long.*

And he still did, even if his mind was scrambling.

He knew it wasn't Penny's fault that she'd had to go away again. Hell, she'd been the most heartbroken of all when she'd been called up again.

But part of him knew it was going to be hard all over again. That there was a chance he could go back to that dark place he'd fallen into while she'd been away last time.

What he'd done, the way he'd hurt her, had spiked him back into action. Pulled him from the pain, but he was struggling, too. *Hurting, too.*

Because he'd broken his own heart as well as Penny's when he'd woken up to the consequences of being with another woman. It had all been too much. Not having Penny, trying to raise Gabby on his own while running a new business, leaving the navy behind and adjusting to being so darn alone that he'd wondered how he managed to breathe sometimes. To keep his head above water.

He'd gone from flying high in the navy as a pilot, surrounded by other men, *friends,* and with every day presenting an exciting challenge.

To living in suburbia as a solo dad.

Penny stirred beside him, turning her face into the pillow and rolling half her body away.

Daniel slipped his lower arm from between them and used it to brace his weight as he eased himself from the bed. As much as he wanted to lie there with her, the last thing he needed was Penny waking and feeling uncomfortable.

"Daddy?"

Daniel only had one foot out of the bed when he heard Gabby. She was standing in the door, hair all mussed up and a smile on her face. Her eyes were still bleary from sleep and she was clutching her favorite furry toy under her arm. A floppy-eared bunny that had seen better days.

"Happy birthday, sweetheart," he said.

Gabby padded over quietly, rubbing at her eyes with one fisted hand. She looked at him, then at Penny, then back at him again.

He wondered what she was thinking.

Penny sat up, like she'd been jolted awake.

"Gabby?" she asked, blinking furiously as she struggled to wake up.

Daniel sat back down on the bed, on top of the covers, and patted the spot between them. "Up you come."

Gabby didn't need to be asked twice. She climbed up the bed, wriggling into the pillows as she sat between them.

Daniel tried not to watch as Penny ran a hand through her hair, trying to tame her usually straight locks into compliance. But he couldn't *not* look at the smile on her face as Gabby touched her arm.

"Is it really my birthday today?" she asked, like she wasn't sure if it was a dream or not.

Daniel laughed, bending down to press a kiss to her cheek. She squirmed but didn't stop smiling.

"Sure is, kiddo," he said, grinning at Penny over their daughter's head as she laughed, too. "And I heard a rumor that you might like a few presents?"

She squealed. "Yes!"

He looked away as Penny adjusted the top of her camisole, not wanting to see her bare skin or even think about the fact they'd shared a bed.

Daniel rolled half off the bed and reached beneath it, pulling out a few small, wrapped gifts before swinging back up to give them to Gabby.

"These," he said, holding them out of her reach

for a second to watch the excitement blur across her face, "are for you. Happy birthday, Gabby."

She eagerly reached for them, ripping into one straight away.

"I'm just going to get some breakfast," he said, slipping out of bed. "You open these with Mommy and I'll be right back."

Gabby hardly looked up, she was so excited about her presents, but Penny met his gaze. He gave her a wink and a smile, hoping she'd realize what he was up to.

So much had happened yesterday they hadn't even had a chance to talk about gifts, but he'd made a big effort this year, so he didn't expect anyone to be disappointed.

Gabby's laughter and excited chatter followed him as he hot-footed it to the garage.

He couldn't wait to see the look on Gabby's face when she saw her main present.

Penny folded her arm around Gabby and pulled her close. She inhaled the sweet smell of her hair, enjoyed the tiny warm body pressed against hers.

Paper was strewn across the bed, and Gabby was transfixed with looking at her things.

"I have something else for you," Penny told

her, reaching for a small package she had placed beside the bed before climbing in the night before.

It was small, but beautifully wrapped. She'd purchased it on a layover on the way home.

"What is it?" Gabby fingered the square present, like she wasn't sure what could be in there. What could be so small.

"Open it and see."

Gabby didn't rip the pink paper. Instead she tugged at the silver bow and slid her little finger beneath the tape. The way a grown-up would, as if she sensed that there was something special inside.

Gabby looked up wide-eyed as she opened it, before staring at the present within.

"It's a charm bracelet," Penny told her, taking it from the box and fastening it around Gabby's wrist. "There are five charms on it now, and every birthday and Christmas I'll buy you another to add to it."

Gabby held up her wrist to look at the charms. "Thanks, Mommy."

Penny pulled her closer for a cuddle and tried not to cry. Her own mother had given her a charm bracelet when she was ten, and Penny had been wanting to do the same for Gabby since she was born. She was probably still too young to have one, but she didn't care. When Penny missed her mother more than usual sometimes, she still fastened her own back on her wrist.

"Drum roll, please." Daniel's playful tone echoed down the hall.

Gabby leaped up, jumping up and down on the bed as if it were a trampoline.

What…?

Gabby gasped as Daniel wheeled in a brand-new pink bike, complete with flowing streamers tied to the handlebars. Gabby's squeal told them she loved it.

"Happy birthday, Gabs. This is from me and your mom."

Gabby leaped from the bed and grabbed on to the handlebars like she was never going to let go.

"Can I ride it?"

Daniel raised an eyebrow at her.

"How about we get dressed first, then we can take it outside," Penny suggested.

"And you'll need to get your new matching pink helmet from the table first, too," Daniel told her.

Gabby sprinted off to find her helmet, leaving Daniel standing forlorn with the bike.

"That's a seriously good present, Danny," Penny said.

As soon as his nickname fell from her mouth she felt a burning flush hit her cheeks. She hadn't said his nickname, the name that *only she called him,* since she'd been home.

Somehow, sitting in bed, in their bedroom, and calling him Danny felt too intimate.

"Can I tempt you with breakfast?" he asked.

Penny tugged the sheets a little tighter around herself. "That would be great," she said honestly. Her stomach rumbled in agreement.

"Waffles still your favorite?"

She closed her eyes and leaned back for a beat. "Yeah, they are."

And they were only her favorite because Daniel had made them for her every Sunday since they'd been together, whenever they were both off-duty at home.

"Do you remember the first time I made you waffles?" he asked, voice low, almost hoarse.

Penny nodded, fighting the smile that so desperately wanted to escape to trace her lips.

She remembered, all right. How could she ever forget?

"It was the first morning we'd woken up together," she remembered out loud. "I stayed tucked up in bed while you went out to the store."

Daniel leaned against the wall, his eyes never leaving hers. It was as if he was caressing her with his gaze, with his memories. His face showed an openness and warmth that she couldn't turn away from.

"I made you waffles with maple syrup."

"With strawberries, melon and blueberries on the side," she finished, too carried away with the memories to stop.

"We had a pot of coffee and we sat out in the sun, talking about everything and anything."

Penny didn't know what to say. Or where to look.

Daniel was still watching her, conveying so much feeling in his gaze that she could feel a slithering-snake kind of nervousness building in her belly.

"Are you coming?" Gabby called at the top of her lungs.

They continued to stare at one another in silence.

Until Daniel broke the quiet that had fallen around them.

"Yeah, in a sec, honey."

Penny folded the sheet beneath her forefinger and thumb.

The air around them seemed limited, like there wasn't enough of it in the room to service both their lungs.

"We should go," she said.

Daniel hesitated, before sighing and tightening his grip on the bike.

"Yeah."

"Give me a couple of minutes and I'll be right out."

Daniel turned, before stopping, the rise then fall of his shoulders signaling there was something left he wanted to say. That he had something else on his mind.

"We had some great times, Penny."

She nodded, even though he couldn't see her. His back was still turned.

"The best," she whispered.

And they were memories she'd never be able to let go of for as long as she lived.

The house was full of guests before Penny had had time to catch her breath. Other little kids, friends she hadn't seen in far too long and Daniel's family.

"Pen!"

She spun and found herself in the arms of one of her closest friends. "Sammi! It's been way too long."

They hugged tight.

"You look great. You know, for being in the desert so long."

Penny laughed. "Yeah, well, there's something to be said for being out in the open all day."

Sammi kept her tight against her, arm wrapped around her shoulders.

"How are you, really?" her friend asked.

Penny dropped her head to rest on Sammi's shoulder. "Really?" she asked, sighing. "I'm coping, but it's hard. I don't know what's going to happen."

Sammi didn't say anything back, she didn't need to. They'd been friends long enough to just *be*.

"We're here for you. Don't you ever forget that, okay?"

Penny snuggled closer into her shoulder, then raised her head. "You're the best."

"Who's the best?"

Gabby poked her head between them.

"Hey, birthday girl!" Penny grabbed hold of her hands and gave her an impromptu twirl. "You been showing off that shiny new bike?"

Gabby bounced on the spot like only an exuberant child can.

"Yeah. The boys are *way* jealous."

Penny and Sammi both laughed.

"I'm going to go help your dad in the kitchen. Why don't you go play?"

"Is it almost cake time?"

Penny ruffled her hair then gave her a gentle push away. "Almost. Now go have fun."

Sammi squeezed her hand before she walked away.

"You're the strongest person I know, Pen. You *will* get through this."

Penny brushed a tear from the corner of her eye and made for the kitchen.

Only to run smack-bang into the man she was crying over.

"Oops." Daniel did a fast sideways maneuver and jumped out of her way, a plate of goodies held above his head.

"Sorry, Danny, I mean—" she stuttered, wishing she could stop herself from calling him that. "Do you, ah, need any help? I didn't mean to leave you for so long."

He grinned. "Everyone's so excited to have you home. Go enjoy yourself."

The way he looked at her, his dark hair skimming his forehead as it flicked forward slightly, made her want to twist away and run. But she stood her ground, trying to be brave.

"You want one before the kids get their sticky mitts on them?"

He lowered the tray and held it out. Penny reached for a mini hot dog and dipped it in the sauce.

"I'm so full from breakfast still."

Daniel looked up at her with such warmth in his eyes he almost made her choke on the meat.

"How about you put the candles in the cake and I'll ferry this out into the room?" he suggested.

Penny walked a few steps backward and watched him go.

Wishing she had the nerve to pull him in for a kiss and steal his breath away. To see if it still felt the same, to see if she could forget.

To see if what they'd once had was still there.

But she didn't. Instead she bit the inside of her mouth and started fossicking through the nearest drawer for candles.

"They're in the top drawer."

Daniel's deep voice made her hands still. Caught her unaware.

Penny froze as he hovered behind her. Daniel's large frame had stopped, paused behind her so close she could feel him, could lean back and find herself pressed against his hard chest.

She shut her eyes. Didn't know what to do.

Was powerless to stop the pull of her body toward the man she knew so intimately.

"Here," he whispered, placing his hand over hers and guiding it to the right drawer.

Penny didn't fight his touch. Couldn't. Because it had been so long since she'd had this kind of contact with a man, with her man.

Daniel's breath was soft on the back of her neck, made her skin prickle all over.

She could see the candles, but his hand hadn't moved and she was powerless to move her own away from his.

"Penny," he whispered, transferring his hold to her wrist and turning it over in his grip so that she had to turn.

She didn't say his name back, but she didn't resist either. Turned as he gently spun her.

To find herself facing his chest, her eyes level with his collarbone. Penny lifted her gaze slowly, up his neck, to his jaw and then to his eyes.

The need, the desire she saw there, made her step back, her bottom hitting the kitchen bench.

But Daniel was too quick, had seen it coming, and cupped her waist with both his hands to stop her from getting away.

"Let me kiss you, Penny," he whispered, his voice low and husky.

She didn't know what to say. She wanted it and yet she didn't, but her body betrayed her. Her mouth parted, responding to the call his was putting out.

"Danny," she whispered, wanting to tell him *no* yet failing badly.

He bent, mouth so close to crushing hers.

Penny's head dipped back, her body dangerously close to Daniel's.

"Daddy?"

They both froze.

Daniel pulled back, his hands sliding from Penny's waist to slowly hang back at his sides.

She gripped the bench behind her, legs shaking.

"Yeah," he said gruffly.

"What are you doing to Mommy? Isn't it cake time yet?"

"We're, um, looking for candles," Penny said, cheeks burning at being caught by their daughter.

"Oh, okay," Gabby said, skipping out of the room.

Daniel turned almost-black eyes at her and smiled.

"I'll get those candles," she said, needing the distance from him, hoping he stepped backward rather than toward her.

"I'll, ah, take the rest of the food out."

She listened to Daniel pick up another tray and walk out.

It only just gave her enough time to flop forward on the bench, her elbows resting on it so she could cradle her head in her hands for a moment.

Coming home was harder than she'd expected it to be. So hard it made her feel as if a ton of concrete was trapped on her chest, crushing her lungs.

She'd expected to be so angry with Daniel that she wouldn't even be able to look at him. Disgusted with what he'd done.

But now she was here, it was the memories of what they'd had that kept playing through her mind.

She still couldn't forgive him, but forgetting their past seemed to be as difficult as forgetting what he'd done.

Penny forced her head up and reached for the candles. She chose the five prettiest ones from the pack and pushed them carefully into the cake.

Daniel had asked for a chance to prove himself last night, to pretend for Gabby's sake.

She hadn't wanted to hear the details before. To talk about what had gone wrong in their marriage.

Maybe she hadn't been there enough for him.

Hadn't been emotionally available enough to truly understand what he'd gone through leaving the navy. Just because they'd both joined to get their qualifications, it didn't mean they didn't both love what they did. Hadn't learned to love the camaraderie of their careers, even if they had only signed up for the minimum term each.

But if the constant tug within her chest was anything to go by, she owed it to him, herself and to Gabby to be brave.

She hadn't made a career for herself as a sergeant in the United States Army by being a coward.

## CHAPTER SEVEN

PENNY picked up the last paper plate off the floor and dumped it in the trash. She had no idea how so few children could make such a huge mess.

"All done in here?"

She looked up, blowing out her breath so hard that tendrils of hair flew up around her face. "Finally."

Daniel collected the garbage bag and tied the top in a knot. "She had a great time."

Penny collected a glass to put in the dishwasher. "So did I."

He looked thoughtful before carrying the bag into the kitchen.

"Penny, I know you want to spend time with Gabby, but…"

She put the glass down and spread her hands out on the bench. "What is it?"

It was unlike him to be unsure with his words. Daniel was usually forthright, never hesitated.

"I was wondering if you'd like to go away. Even just for a night." His voice was rapid, he was talking too fast.

Where did he want to take her? And why?

"Daniel, I only have six days left, I can't leave her."

His face crumpled before the strength returned and he stood taller, looked confident and composed. The man-in-uniform kind of Daniel she was used to.

"One night," he said, stepping forward so that he was as close as he could be to her from the other side of the bench. "Let me take us away somewhere for one night."

She physically squirmed on the spot, unsure.

"Daniel, I don't want you to get the wrong idea…"

He shook his head. "Please, Penny, this is really important to me."

She didn't want to say yes. Or maybe she did.

Hell, she'd been so confused since she'd been home she hardly knew *what* she was thinking. What she wanted.

"Pen?"

"I don't know what to say," she replied honestly.

"There's something else I want to ask you." His voice was soft now, careful.

Penny sucked in a breath and bent to place the glass she'd held before in the dishwasher. She flicked the switch.

Then looked up.

"I completely understand why you don't want to leave Gabby, but we need to spend time together."

She waited as he paused, not sure what he was getting at.

"Let me take you out on a date."

Oh, my.

"A date?"

Daniel looked suddenly serious, solemn even.

"This could be it for us, Penny, and I can't let you go without a fight."

"Daniel…" Sweat clammed her forehead, instantly made her feel claustrophobic beneath her sweater.

It had been a long time since she'd been on a date.

"I know we're living together, but I want to spend time with you, just the two of us. I think we need to give *us* a real shot."

She fought the barbed words in her throat that wanted to sting him.

Penny hated that they even had to try. That they'd lost what they had. But saying that all over again wasn't going to help the situation. And she didn't want to be bitter. Didn't want to fight, yell, argue. It wasn't her, and she wanted to preserve her dignity.

Even if all the people in her life that she loved already knew the truth about her marriage.

"I'm not sure it's such a good idea, Daniel. I don't want to fight with you."

He reached for her hand across the counter. Traced his fingertips across hers and played them softly along the top of her hand, then around her wrist, before pulling away and tilting her chin with his hand.

The touch felt intimate. Way too intimate.

She wanted to push him away and tell him he didn't have the right to touch her body, her face, like that anymore.

But she also wanted to remember what it felt like to be touched. To be caressed by the hand of a man who had once loved her.

"It doesn't have to be anything more than two

people who know each other spending time to-gether," he said, his voice gruff. "We can go out once Gabby's in bed, and it won't impact at all on your spending time with her."

"We'd need a babysitter," she mumbled.

Daniel chuckled. "All taken care of. My mom's ready and waiting to be called upon."

Penny shut her eyes, took a deep breath and opened them again with a confidence that sur-prised her. Of course she was.

"Yes."

He raised an eyebrow. "Yes?"

Penny tucked her hair behind her ears and raised her eyes to look at Daniel.

"Yes to your date," she told him, with a bravery she didn't truly feel. "I didn't marry you to be divorced before my thirtieth birthday."

He smiled. Except she wasn't finished.

"I also didn't expect to be dealing with a hus-band who'd been unfaithful and broken my heart by then either."

The words were hard to push out, but then so was seeing the crushed look that passed across Daniel's face.

She had to say what was on her mind, though.

If she didn't, they'd never be able to move forward. Perhaps that's where they'd gone wrong—not being honest and up-front enough about how they felt. About the problems they were facing.

"I'm sorry, Pen," he said, shaking his head sorrowfully. "I'm so, so sorry for what I did."

She smiled tightly. "I accept your apology, Daniel, I do. But it doesn't mean that we can ever go back to normal. That we could ever expect *us* to work again."

"I want it to," he said. "God, Penny, I want to be back to the way things were."

For the first time since she could remember, Daniel had tears in his eyes. Tears threatening to spill down his cheeks. Not since her mother's funeral, maybe since Gabby's birth, did she recall seeing his tears.

She fought the emotion in her own throat, determined to keep her composure. At least until she was in the private sanctuary of the bathroom where she could sob quietly in peace.

Maybe they should have just argued. Maybe they needed to have a rip-roaring row and vent their anger and frustration. But that wasn't her, *she didn't want that to be her,* and she certainly didn't want to behave like that when her daughter was asleep down the hall.

"So when's our date?" she asked, forcing herself to smile. To stop the conversation from getting too heavy. Because she wasn't ready to go there yet.

"Tomorrow night," he said.

She reached for the dishcloth to give the bench a final wet down.

"Anywhere in particular?"

"Yeah." Daniel's face lit up with a smile. "Pedro's," he told her, head angled slightly to the side. "I thought I'd take you back to Pedro's."

The look on her face ignited something within Daniel that he hadn't felt in a long time.

Made him feel alive again. When for the last while, for as long as he could remember, he'd felt like a flag at half-mast. Like he was just below the surface and couldn't quite claw his way back up.

But Penny was slowly reigniting the flame within him that hadn't burned for a long time.

Slowly making him feel like himself again.

"Pedro's," she stuttered, her eyes as large as a cat's in the dark. "Are you sure?"

He thrummed his fingers across the bench for something to do. Because he didn't know how else to rid himself of the nervous energy vibrating through his body.

"I'm positive," he said, hoping she wasn't going to change her mind. "It's the first restaurant I ever took you to for dinner."

"I know," she whispered. "It was our first real date."

Her gaze was sad, but the gentle curve of her mouth, the hint of a smile, was the encouragement he needed.

"We fell in love that night, Penny," he said, walking around to stand in front of her, to touch her hair and push it over her shoulder. "It was also the place where I proposed to you."

She gulped, he could see the movement of her throat.

They were standing close, but he wasn't going to push his luck. Daniel wanted to know that she remembered. That even though he might have been aloof in the past about things like anniversaries, he'd never forgotten the things that mattered.

"And it's the place I want to take you tomorrow night, because it might be the place we start to fall in love all over again," he said, his voice laced with emotion.

In the past, he'd always told her he loved her. But maybe he hadn't made enough of an effort. Maybe they'd just started to take each other for granted, to coast through their marriage rather than work on it. Maybe he should never have kept his feelings buried, should have been honest with her instead of trying to pretend that everything was okay between them.

That stopped here.

"We've got a lot of stuff to talk about, Penny, but tomorrow night I want to just enjoy one another. I want us to remember why we started dating in the first place. Why we got married."

She looked up at him, reached for his hand, squeezed it then stepped back.

*Why we should stay married,* he wanted to say.

But he didn't say anything else because he didn't need to. The look on Penny's face, the moistness of her eyes, told him that she knew.

That he didn't have to tell her why tomorrow night was so important.

"You want to watch a movie tonight?"

Her question took him by surprise.

"Yeah," he said, not able to stop the grin as it hit his face. "I'd love to."

Penny's face softened, visibly relaxed. "My choice or yours?"

"Considering you haven't been able to pick a movie for the last year, I'm gonna let you have the honor."

"Hope you're up for a romantic comedy, then?"

Daniel could tell she was making a huge effort.

He shrugged. He couldn't care less what they watched, so long as she was up for doing *something* together.

Penny tucked her feet up beneath herself on the sofa. She was watching the movie but she wasn't. Her eyes roamed the screen but her senses were focused on the man beside her.

They'd been sitting there for an hour, side by side yet not touching.

She was glad. The last thing she wanted was to complicate her feelings any further.

After what had happened earlier…

"Another glass of wine?"

Penny shook her head. "I'm fine, thanks."

He pushed up to his feet and reached for both their glasses. "How about a hot chocolate, then? Coffee?"

"I'm guessing you're not enjoying the movie?" Penny laughed at the pained expression on Daniel's face. "Looking for a chance to escape?"

He looked meek. "You got me."

Penny reached for the remote and hit Pause. "It's not that great anyway."

He blew out a sigh of what she guessed was relief. "Are you sure? I don't mind watching the whole thing."

She shrugged. "I'm pretty tired, Daniel. Maybe we should call it a night."

Daniel looked like he might have preferred to suffer through the movie than go to bed early, but he didn't say.

"I'll be down soon," he said.

Penny gave him a small smile and stretched. She *was* tired. It had been a long day catching up with everyone, giving Gabby as much attention as she could. Being upbeat even though she was breaking inside at the thought of leaving again so soon after arriving home.

Was shattered at knowing her days were numbered and she'd be leaving all she loved behind and getting back on a plane by Monday.

"Daddy?"

Penny stopped dead in her tracks.

Gabby's tiny voice echoed out from her room.

"It's Mommy."

She heard quiet sobbing as she entered, hurried to flick on the lamp beside Gabby's bed.

"Sweetheart, are you okay?"

"I want Daddy." She was crying, eyes filled with rapidly falling tears.

Penny bent to wrap her arms around her daughter, to cradle her head and comfort her.

Only to be shrugged off, Gabby's arms being pulled up toward her eyes, knees drawn up to her chest.

"I want my daddy," she whispered as she cried.

Penny didn't know what to do. Whether to force the issue or to call for Daniel. To hold her daughter and comfort her even if she wasn't the first person she'd called for. Or to give her what she wanted.

Because what was the point in Gabby getting used to calling for her mother if she wasn't going to be here?

She sucked in a big breath. Even so, she wanted to be the one to comfort her. "Honey, I'm here. Mommy's here."

Was it so bad to want to care for her own daughter?

Gabby pulled her arms away and pushed her palms down flat into the bed. When she looked up, her brown eyes were like saucers, glimmering with dampness, her cheeks pink, hair mussed up all around her face.

"But I don't want you," she sobbed. "I want my dad."

Penny's heart physically shattered into a million shards. Tears filled her own eyes, drowned her tear ducts.

"Everything okay down here?"

Gabby began to wail, the noise subsiding only when Daniel flopped down on the bed beside her and cradled her tiny body against his large one.

Penny couldn't watch. Couldn't deal with the pain of knowing her daughter didn't want her.

Her husband hadn't wanted her, had been unfaithful when she needed him the most, and now her daughter didn't want her, didn't need her, either.

"Pen…"

She shook her head, glaring at Daniel with tear-filled eyes even though she knew he didn't deserve her anger. It wasn't his fault that Gabby wanted him and not her.

He couldn't help the way Gabby was behaving. And neither could Gabby. She was used to her father, *loved her father,* and had relied on him for months while her mother had been a memory, someone to look forward to seeing again one day.

These past months, Daniel had been her everything.

Daniel had been Gabby's entire world.

"Penny, stay," he whispered, chin resting on Gabby's head.

*No.* She felt like an intruder just being here.

Like she had no place here anymore.

"I need some fresh air." She expelled the words before the need to cry overwhelmed her so much she doubted she'd be able to speak. Would be able to keep her body upright.

Daniel's eyes pleaded with her as she walked backward then fled down the hall.

But she didn't need comforting, she needed to be alone.

Daniel gently eased his arm from beneath Gabby's shoulders, holding his breath as he waited to see if she would wake.

She didn't, her body relaxed and floppy with slumber as he tucked the covers up to just under her chin.

He dropped a kiss to her cheek and tiptoed out of the room, his legs aching from the tail end of a cramp in his calf muscles after being tucked up on the small bed with his daughter.

Now he needed to find Penny.

He didn't know where she'd gone, what she was feeling, what he would even say to her when he found her.

But one thing was sure—he needed to talk to her.

Because she was alone now and he knew what being alone felt like.

Because he'd been so alone when she'd left, had been on the verge of having a breakdown from suddenly being back home, a single dad, having lost the camaraderie he'd enjoyed his entire adult life being in the navy. From walking away from what he *loved*—being in the air, the feeling of being on top of the world in a helicopter.

And no matter how long they put this off, there were words that had to be said. He'd wanted to delay it, to stall this conversation for at least a day or two, but now he didn't have a choice.

No fancy date night and drawing on happy memories from the past was going to heal their marriage if they kept skirting around their problems.

He'd tried to convince himself otherwise, but he was wrong.

Daniel peeked into their bedroom, knowing she wasn't in there before he even looked. He'd heard the back door click shut not long after she'd walked out of the room.

He found his shoes, pulled them on and reached for a sweater.

It wasn't as if he could leave Gabby in the house alone, but he could walk around outside, see if he could spot her in the street from their yard.

Daniel swung the door open and nearly tripped his way to the bottom step.

Penny hadn't gone far.

She was sitting, body hunched, sobbing quietly in the dark. Perched on the cold concrete step. Alone.

"Oh, Penny." His voice was low, husky with an emotion he couldn't explain. Seeing her sitting like that, so sad and alone, twisted him up inside.

She didn't look up.

"You must be freezing." He pulled off the hooded sweater he'd only just put on and wrapped it around her shoulders. It looked huge on her small frame, but it would take the chill away. "Come inside."

Her body was shaking.

He didn't know if it was the cold, because she was so upset, or both.

Daniel sighed and dropped to sit beside her. The step was narrow so he was pressed against her, thigh to thigh, knee to knee.

She didn't protest. Didn't try to move away.

"Penny, you're cold," he said, putting his arm around her shoulders, wanting to warm her with his own body. "I know you're upset, but you need to come inside."

"No," she whispered, voice unsteady. "Leave me, Daniel."

Her words went deeper than talking about right here, right now. She might not have meant anything by it, but he felt that walking away now to leave her alone and sad outside in the dark would mean walking away for good.

"Penny, Gabby does love you. Please don't think any differently."

She didn't say anything straight away. Sucked in deep breath after deep breath, as if trying to compose herself.

"I know." She cleared her throat, voice stronger the second time. "I know, I do, but it doesn't make it any easier."

"It's been hard on me, too, Penny. I know that might sound like a cop-out to you, but it has."

Something flashed through her gaze then, something he could see even in the dark.

Anger maybe. Or perhaps disbelief.

"But you've *been here,* Daniel. You've been here and I've been away." She shook her head. "It's not fair, Daniel, none of this is fair."

He stood, not wanting to sit any longer.

Not sure if he was ready to have this conversation yet after all.

"You think it's been easy for me?" he said in a low voice, refusing to let anger creep into his tone. Unable to shoulder all the blame any longer. "You think it was easy for me to pretend to you like everything was okay when I was dying inside here? When I didn't know how to be a full-time dad, when all I knew was how to be a pilot? I'd give up anything for my family, but leaving the navy behind was nothing like *easy.*"

Penny looked up then, too, drew her body up tall even though she was still seated.

"Let's not talk about *easy,* Daniel." Her tone was cold, angry. Like she hadn't heard anything he'd said except that one word. "Don't even get me started on *easy.*"

Fury built within him until he felt like a jug about to boil over. A volcano about to blow its top after centuries of being dormant.

"And what exactly is that meant to mean?"

The tears were gone now, only to be replaced by a strong, calm anger that made him realize why she was so good at her job. Why his young wife had made sergeant. Why the United States Army was so darn keen to keep her in their service.

"I take it you were pretty easy the night you cheated on me." She spat the words at him now. "Or have you forgotten about that already? Forgotten that when all we had was trust, when I was on the other side of the world and couldn't do anything about it, you decided to throw our marriage away like it wasn't worth the paper it was written on."

"How dare you." His body was shaking. "How dare you make out like our marriage means nothing to me?"

"How *dare* I?" Penny jumped to her feet then. "I have never been unfaithful, Daniel. In all the years we've been together, I have never once been tempted by another man."

They glared at one another. Yeah, he'd done something stupid, hated that he'd hurt her, but she didn't understand. He hated himself for what he'd done. But he was hurting, too.

"You left me here, Penny. You left me and I had nothing."

She laughed. "Nothing? You had our daughter, you had your family and you had your job."

"No," he said, shaking his head. Sad now instead of angry. "I had no wife, I had to figure out how to look after a four-year-old girl on my own, and I had to deal with losing my identity. The navy had been my whole life, Penny, and it would have been different to give that up and come home to you. But it was the first time in my life that I've ever felt alone. Every time we spoke I pretended like everything was okay, but it wasn't. I've never felt so sad and alone in all my life, okay? But I wanted to shield you from it and so I suffered on my own. I kept my mouth shut."

She was still glaring at him, but she didn't say a thing.

"Yeah, I stuffed up, but I would do anything to take that back. I've never, ever wanted to hurt you, and if I hadn't been so damn drunk, so miserable, so lonely, I…"

"Am I meant to feel sorry for you?"

He reached for her hand, wanting this fight to be over. Wanting her to understand. Not knowing what to say or how to say it. Wishing he'd kept it all to himself again.

"If I could take it back, I would. I know it was wrong, but at the time, hell, I don't know. I felt like I was sinking, at the bottom of a well with no hope of fighting my way to the top. I was stupid-drunk, I know that's no excuse, but I swear on my life that I'll never, ever hurt you again."

"My mother fell pregnant with me to a man she thought loved her. And what did he do once she told him? He left her. Because he had a wife he'd never told her about." She crossed her arms tightly across her chest. "I grew up without a father as the result of infidelity. Your own father cheated on your mother and left you without a dad to rely on."

He stared at her.

"Don't ever compare me to my father." He heard the coolness of his tone but was powerless to stop it. He despised the man.

"I grew up believing that I'd never find a man I could trust. That I could love. Because of what my mother had told me about my own father." Tears started to fall down her cheeks again as she spoke. "But then I met you, Daniel, and I trusted *you.* I gave you my heart and never once doubted your love, or that you'd always be there for me. I loved you so much that it hurt sometimes, and now I have to think about that man whom I trusted so much with another woman. With his arms, his hands, *his lips* on another woman's. And it's something I don't know how to forget."

"I'm sorry, Penny. I know I've hurt you, but…"

"Screw you, Daniel."

Penny spun around, his sweater falling from her shoulders, hair swinging as she flung the door open.

He stood still. He couldn't do anything else.

In the ten years he'd been with Penny, in all that time of knowing her, he'd never seen such anger in her gaze. Never felt the sting like a slap to his cheek of Penny firing such venom-laced words at him.

*Never.* Not as a nineteen-year-old and not as a grown woman.

Daniel bent to retrieve his sweater, pulled it on then let himself out the gate. He needed to take a walk, even just down the street.

And he needed to give Penny some breathing space to gather her own thoughts, too.

Their discussion hadn't gone well, but then he'd never really expected it to.

Although he'd never thought it would be quite that bad.

Penny was furious. Mind-jarring, body-shaking, wild kind of furious.

How dare he? How could he think that there was any excuse for the way he'd behaved? The way he'd hurt her?

She'd been away on tour with a huge number of men. All types of different guys, plenty of them handsome and charming, but she'd never once even considered giving in to temptation. No matter how sad or lonely she was.

Because her marriage meant too much to her.

Was she meant to feel sorry for him? Think it was okay that he'd been with another woman because he'd been lonely?

She would have traded anything not to have to go away again. To be here with Gabby instead of serving overseas. She'd done her time, fulfilled her duty, and now she wanted to come home. No matter how much she loved her unit, liked being part of a team and making a difference.

And Daniel was wrong. *She knew exactly what it meant to be lonely.*

She'd been living *lonely* ever since she'd flown out and left her husband standing beside her daughter. Looked over her shoulder and seen the pair of them holding hands while she had to board a plane and leave them for months on end. When she'd never expected to have to go on tour again. When her contract said that after four years of service she'd be free to be a civilian again.

She'd miss the people she served with, too, but she'd trade it all for being right back here at home.

Penny threw a pillow and a blanket out onto the sofa and hoped Daniel got the message.

Pretending or not, she had no intention of sharing a bed with him. Not tonight, and maybe not ever again.

# CHAPTER EIGHT

A KNOCK echoed out down the hall. Penny looked up. She was sitting on the sofa reading to Gabby. The last thing she needed was a visitor. Her head was still pounding from the night she'd spent tossing and turning, eyes no doubt verging on seriously bloodshot.

"I'll get it!" Daniel called out.

She glimpsed him as he walked past the living room door, jeans slung low on his waist, towel still in his hand as he rubbed at his damp hair.

Penny wished she hadn't seen him. The last thing she needed was to be reminded of how good he looked bare. The golden color of his flat torso, the breadth of his shoulders.

Clearly leaving the navy hadn't taken a toll on his appearance.

"Oh, hey," she heard him say.

Gabby jumped up. "Is that Grandma?"

Penny strained her ears but couldn't hear. "I don't know, hon. Why don't you go take a look?"

She watched as her daughter bounded off down the hall, returning less than a minute later towing her grandmother.

"Hi, Penny."

"Oh. Hi, Vicki," she responded.

She ran her hands over her rumpled jeans before playing anxiously with her ponytail. She was suddenly conscious that the house was a mess. That she didn't even have dinner on yet.

But she'd been having such a lovely time with Gabby, Daniel had spent the afternoon at work, and she was only talking to him when she had to, to make sure Gabby didn't figure out there was anything wrong. She hadn't even thought about what they were going to eat.

"I, ah, didn't know you were coming over." Why hadn't Daniel told her? "I'll rustle up something for dinner if you're staying?"

Vicki sent a confused look at Daniel.

"I'm sorry, darling, was tonight supposed to be a surprise?"

Daniel groaned, the noise only just audible. "I forgot to cancel."

*Great.*

"Daniel…" Penny started.

Vicki frowned before bending to talk to Gabby. "Why don't you run and get some of your presents to show me again," Vicki asked her. "Silly Grandma's already forgotten what you got for your birthday."

Gabby ran off with a smile on her face. Vicki's face was more solemn.

"I don't know what's happened here today, but I'm not going to stand around and let you mope," she said to both of them, her voice stern. "I'm here now so you may as well go out and enjoy yourselves."

Penny held up her hands. "I'm sorry to waste your time, Vicki, but I think dinner's off the cards."

Daniel didn't say anything. He looked at the ground, before raising his eyes slowly to meet Penny's gaze.

"Are you sure?"

She glared at him. "Yes." She had no intention of going through with their date night. "Besides, Gabby seems to have a bit of a cold or something coming on."

Vicki looked deflated. Like she'd been looking forward to seeing the pair of them go out.

"What time was the booking, Daniel?" his mother asked.

"Seven."

Vicki took a step forward and touched Penny's shoulder. "You've got an hour to get yourself ready," she said, voice low. "Can you not both put aside your differences and enjoy a meal together? You can have your dinner, chat about your daughter and then come home. I'll make Gabby dinner, then put her to bed."

Penny felt her mother-in-law's gentle squeeze to her arm. She looked at Daniel. His gaze was... hopeful.

Penny shut her eyes, thought for half a second, then gave in.

It *would* be nice to have a meal out. To discuss what they were going to do custody-wise once she was home for good. Talk about Gabby and how they were going to deal with her leaving. About telling her what had happened between them, and perhaps even being honest with her about what it was her mother did for a career. Daniel must have told her something, but it was about time they came clean about her being a soldier.

"Pen, why don't you have a shower and think about it?"

She forced a smile on her face. "You know what? Maybe it's not such a bad idea."

So long as it wasn't a date.

Vicki beamed at them both, reaching out for Gabby as she appeared, arms laden with goodies.

"Grandma, you do remember about my bike, don't you?"

"Of course, sweetheart, it was all the other things I needed reminding about."

Penny tried to avoid Daniel's gaze as she went to the bathroom, but it wasn't easy. His eyes followed hers, she could feel them burning into her as if his pupils were laced with acid.

Her stomach churned at the thought of a night out, just the two of them. After their argument last night, the words they'd said, the anger that had blasted between them…she wondered how they'd even manage to sit across from one another for an entire meal.

But maybe it was what they needed, she thought, as she stepped out of her clothes and under the hot stream of water in the shower. They couldn't argue in public. She wouldn't embarrass herself by walking out of a restaurant.

So maybe, just maybe, dinner wouldn't be so bad. They could eat, have a civil conversation and head home, like Vicki had suggested.

Daniel tugged at the edge of his shirt.

He guessed it was nerves making him on edge, but he wasn't sure.

He didn't ever remember being this nervous before. Not before his first flight up in a helicopter. Or the first time he went up solo after joining the navy as a pilot.

He decided to tuck the shirt into his jeans. He'd snuck into the bedroom to grab clothes from his wardrobe while Penny was in the shower. He was still waiting for her to emerge.

"You look lovely."

He smiled at his mother's words, not having realized she'd been watching him. "Yeah, but you have to say that."

Gabby laughed, slapping her hand down with glee on the table.

"I beat you again, Grandma!" she squealed, before coughing.

Daniel exchanged looks with his mother as she put up her hands in defeat. "So you did. But don't forget to cover your mouth when you cough."

Daniel went to sit on the sofa to wait, but his body stuttered to a stop. He didn't even have a chance to ask Gabby how she was feeling.

*Wow.*

"You look fantastic."

He couldn't help but stare as Penny walked into the room. She had on jeans that were so snug he could see almost every contour of her legs, paired with a low-front, slinky looking T-shirt, and she had her favorite leather jacket on, hanging open.

Geez. He'd forgotten how incredible she looked dressed to go out.

And he'd always loved that worn biker-style jacket on her.

"I haven't worn this stuff in forever," she said with a sigh, cheeks flushing ever-so as he watched her. "I hope it's still okay."

Daniel was struggling to stop his jaw from hitting the floor. "You look fantastic, Penny." *Good enough to eat.*

He saw Gabby move from the corner of his eye.

"You okay, hon?" Penny asked.

Their daughter nodded, before moving slowly over to her mother. She took her hand, looking her up and down.

Daniel realized she probably didn't remember Penny ever looking like this.

It was the Penny he knew before they'd gotten married and had Gabby. This was the smoking-hot Penny he'd first fallen in love with.

"You look so pretty, Mommy." Gabby was clearly impressed with her mother. "Like, *really* pretty."

Penny laughed and bent to kiss her on the cheek.

"Will you be okay with Grandma? Are you feeling okay?" She pressed her palm to Gabby's forehead.

Gabby nodded. "Is Daddy going with you?"

He took a step forward, his body recovering from the shock of Penny standing in front of him.

From his wife.

Daniel grabbed his keys. "Yeah, I'm taking Mommy out for dinner."

"Have a nice night, kids," Vicki called from the table.

"We won't be late," Penny told her, walking ahead of Daniel toward the front door.

Daniel ran a step ahead to grab the door for her, to hold it open for Penny to walk through.

"Thanks," she said, eyes flickering over his as he passed.

It was the little things that counted, he knew that. Just like he knew that she'd always liked being treated like a lady. Liked the fact that she could be in a male-dominated career like the army and still feel like a woman when she was home.

Maybe it had been the little things he'd forgotten about. And maybe she had, too.

But tonight, he was going to remember every single little detail.

"I'm really glad we decided to go out," he said, unlocking the car by remote as they walked.

Penny looked over her shoulder at him, eyes twinkling his way. There was a softness there he hadn't seen since the day of Gabby's party.

"Me, too," she replied.

And from the look on her face, the openness he saw there, he knew she meant it.

Daniel jumped out of the driver's side and moved quickly to open Penny's door. If she was surprised, she didn't show it, but she did manage to avoid taking his hand as she stepped out onto the sidewalk.

He watched as she tilted her head back to look at the front of the restaurant. It was an old building, rustic but pleasant, with a modest, solid timber door hiding stairs that led up to the restaurant. Wrought-iron placed over the windows was softened with pots of bright-colored flowers.

"Hasn't changed a bit," she said, sighing.

"That's what I love about it," he told her, locking the car and holding the heavy restaurant door open.

She paused before walking past him. "Have you been here lately?"

"You mean while you've been away?"

She nodded.

Hell, no. Never.

"I'd never come here without you, Penny. It's always been our place." Daniel couldn't stop the huskiness in his tone. He'd never even considered coming here without her.

"I don't even think I've been out for dinner since you left," he told her, following her up the stairs. "To Mom's place and through the drive-through with Gabby, but nowhere like this."

The scent of Spanish food hit Daniel's nostrils as they left the staircase behind and found themselves in the middle of the restaurant. Every table was full, the atmosphere happy and lively.

"It feels like so long."

Daniel looked up at Penny's words. It looked as if she had tears in her eyes, but he couldn't be sure, didn't want to ask her.

"It has been a long time, Pen. We left it way too long to come back here. To do a lot of things."

Her eyes questioned him but she didn't say anything. They'd been treading on eggshells since their argument the night before.

"Welcome!" A dark-haired waiter appeared with menus and pointed to the only empty table. A small candle blazed in the center, sending a flicker of light out across the tablecloth.

Daniel waited for Penny to be seated before

sitting down himself. He smiled at her across the table and received a tight smile in return.

He knew he had to say something, *do something,* now before things became even more awkward and strained between them.

"Penny..."

"Daniel..."

They both laughed.

"You go," she said, smile genuine now as it hit her eyes.

"I just wanted to say that I'm sorry about last night." He paused, ran a hand through his hair before leaning back in his chair. "I hate arguing and I'm so sorry if I upset you."

She shook her head. Sadly.

"I'm sorry, too, Daniel. It's just, well." This time it was Penny who paused, who looked at her hands before raising her eyes to meet his. "I don't want us to be like this, but I can't help how I feel. I'm still so angry with you, but I do want to get past this."

Hope flickered within him. He almost didn't want to ask what she meant. Didn't want her to elaborate.

But he didn't want to be left hanging, *hoping,* either.

"When you say you want to get past this…"

She leaned back like she hadn't realized how her words had sounded.

"What I mean is that I don't want to ruin our relationship so much that all we can do is fight. We owe Gabby more than that. Hell, we owe ourselves better than that."

There was so much that needed to be said. So much they needed to talk about.

But tonight was about having dinner and putting what had happened behind them. He had hoped it would be a romantic date when he'd first planned it; now he was simply pleased they were sitting down together and talking. Without fighting.

They'd never fought in the past and he hated that they'd been reduced to that now.

He picked up the menu. "Do we even need to look?" he asked.

Penny seemed happy to turn the subject away from them. "No," she said, laughing as she spoke. "Sizzling prawns in garlic to start with, and the slow-cooked lamb shoulder for a main."

He snapped his menu shut and waved over the waiter. "Great choice."

"And wine," she said, visibly relaxing. "I think tonight calls for a good bottle of wine."

Daniel couldn't have agreed more.

"Do you remember that first time we came here?" he asked, not able to help going back into the past.

"Yeah," she said, fingers playing with the edge of her napkin. "I was so nervous, but you won me over with the great food."

He laughed. "Are you sure it was just the food?"

She beamed back at him, like old times for a moment. "Okay, so maybe it was the wine, too."

Daniel bit his tongue as the waiter came back and ordered a bottle of red.

"If I remember correctly, you seemed to like something else about me when we left the restaurant."

Penny gasped, hand shooting up to cover her mouth. "Daniel!"

He shrugged, leaning back in his seat and trying not to laugh at the look on her face. "Hey, you remember the food, I remember the fun outside later. Can you blame me?"

They sat in silence, looking at one another as their wine arrived and both glasses were poured. It was like they were on a tightrope, with no idea which way they would fall, or if they could possibly make it to the other side.

Daniel raised his glass and waited for Penny to do the same, clinking them gently together.

"To having you home," he said.

"To being home," she replied.

Their gazes met across the table as they both sipped.

Daniel could feel the connection they still shared, sense the past they were both remembering in such detail.

The only difference now was that while he'd once been able to reach for his wife across the table and caress her hand, now he was forced to keep his distance. At least physically.

And not for the first time since she'd arrived home, not being able to touch her freely was like a stake being spiked through his heart.

Penny wanted to be angry with Daniel. Hell, he'd hurt her enough last night to make her want to hate him forever.

But that was juvenile. She knew that.

And a bigger part of her wanted to be happy with him, to relax in his company, even if it was simply to enjoy a meal together and talk about Gabby. About being parents. Whatever happened, they were bound by the child they'd created and loved together.

But talking about Gabby wasn't what she wanted.

What she wanted was to somehow find the courage to ask him the hows and whys of what had happened to make him stray.

Because no matter how many times she told herself it wasn't her fault, she couldn't convince herself. And now that she wasn't so angry, Daniel's words from the other night kept playing through her mind.

Leaving the army was going to be harder than she expected it to be. Saying goodbye to her unit, giving up the adrenaline and the sense of achievement…it would all be hard. The problem was she'd never thought about it that deeply, had been so focused on getting home that she hadn't even paused to think how Daniel might have felt giving up being a pilot.

"Penny?"

She glanced up, wineglass cradled in her hand.

"Sorry, I was a million miles away."

"Can I ask you a tough question?"

She swallowed another sip of wine and wished she could drink the whole bottle for confidence. "It depends what you're going to ask me."

Daniel looked thoughtful. His deep brown eyes cast down, dark lashes almost bashful. "I want to know if you would ever have come home if it wasn't for Gabby."

Oh, hell.

"Daniel, I don't know how to answer that."

He reached for her hand across the table. Did it so fast that she didn't have a chance to snatch it from his grip.

And it felt so good. Just like his touch always had. Filling her with a warmth that licked like a flame across her hand, up her arm, tingling into her shoulders.

It was a touch she'd missed every night she'd been away.

"Answer me from your heart."

She shook her head, moving it from side to side, unable to stop the rush of emotions roaring in her ears. "No," she whispered. "No, Daniel, I don't think I would have."

He sighed but didn't let go of her hand, didn't relinquish the contact. Instead his thumb brushed across her palm.

"Well, I'm glad you did come home." He paused before forcing his eyes to meet hers again. "I know we're in a bad place right now, one that we might never recover from, but I don't want to lose you, Pen. Regardless of what happens, I don't want to lose you from my life."

She didn't want to lose him either.

"Hot plates coming through. Enjoy!"

Penny pulled her hand back, away from Daniel's, as the steaming clay dishes were placed in front of them.

"Looks delicious," she said, happy to change the topic. *Not strong enough to go there yet.* "Just like I remembered."

She picked up her knife and fork and cut the first prawn in half. The garlic-infused, sizzling-hot juice begged for her to rip a piece of the fresh crusty bread in half to dunk into it.

Penny's mouth wouldn't stop watering.

"Argh!"

She looked up to see Daniel's mouth flapping open and shut, his fork clattering to the table.

"Ouch!"

Penny laughed, she couldn't not. He looked so comical she almost lost the piece of bread she was holding. "Daniel…"

"It's so hot!"

She looked across to see the adjoining table of people looking at them, but she didn't care. It was so nice to be laughing for the hell of it again.

To not have anything else on her mind other than her husband and his seriously burned mouth.

"Burn your tongue?" she asked as he swallowed an entire glass of water in one gulp.

He glared at her like it was her fault, raising an eyebrow.

"Gee, you think?"

Penny dropped her fork and held her napkin to her mouth. She couldn't have stopped laughing if she tried.

"How is my burning my mouth funny?" he demanded.

She laughed harder, unable to stop herself. The kind of cheek-aching laugh that she hadn't enjoyed in forever.

Daniel went to protest again but couldn't stutter the words out. He started laughing, too. The kind of huge, hiccuping laughs that had tears filling both their eyes.

Her laughter slowed to a sort of hard-to-control gulping, and she was sure everyone in the restaurant must have been watching them by now.

Daniel's lips were still curved into the cheekiest of grins, still touched with laughter.

"How did we get here, Penny?" His words were solemn but his face was still kind. Happy. Despite his burned flesh.

She almost asked him what he meant, but deep down, she knew.

"Did we grow apart?" she asked him. Although she knew in her heart she hadn't grown away from him, even through their long absences. "Did you grow apart from me?"

He looked sad, his expression falling. "I don't want to make excuses, but I think we just spent too long apart. The distance became too great."

She wanted to be angry with him, she did. Sadness, bitterness about what had happened still circled deep within her belly like a vulture over prey. But she was able to control it.

"Daniel, even if you hadn't cheated, do you think it would have been easy? Coming home, both of us, and picking up where we left off? Stepping into the life we'd imagined for so long but hadn't ever really lived?"

The sadness of the smile he gave her told her she was right to ask the question.

After all this time, all those hours and days she'd spent thinking about what had gone wrong, blaming him, when maybe it hadn't been entirely his fault. When maybe his cheating had simply been the tip of a slow-forming iceberg within their marriage that they'd both ignored.

Every day, week or month they had spent together had always been on limited time. They'd both always had to spend long absences from home, sometimes for months.

She wasn't going to forgive him, he'd still made vows to her, promised to remain faithful. But…

"Penny, I've never stopped loving you, but maybe we did spend too long apart," he said, voice low as his hand moved slowly across the table. As if he was asking permission to touch her this time, without wanting to say it out loud. She moved her own hand forward, let him rub his finger across hers. "The longest time we ever spent together was when Gabby was born."

Tears touched her eyes, tickled at the back of her throat.

"So we were always doomed?"

A brightness lit Daniel's eyes, changed his expression, made him look almost fierce.

"No," he said. "You're wrong, Penny." He shook his head before squeezing her hand tight. "I stuffed this up, it's still my fault we've ended up like this. But maybe we should have been more honest about our feelings, instead of trying to pretend everything was always okay to make the other feel good. When you were away and I was home I never wanted to worry you, never wanted to trouble you, and I'm guessing you felt the same when our roles were reversed."

She dropped contact with him, picked up her fork again and speared a prawn. Her appetite had fallen away, there was no longer a hunger growling in her stomach, but she still wanted to eat. Didn't want to waste the beautiful food in front of her.

And she needed time to think.

Because he was right.

"I wish everything had gone to plan, Danny." She slowly ate the prawn, then another, before dunking her bread and eating that, too. "I feel so bitter about my service being extended. I know it's wrong, that I should just get on with it and focus on finishing this tour, but leaving Gabby behind will be so hard this time. And then I start to wonder if we'd have been okay, if none of this would have happened, if my term had finished up when it was supposed to."

His expression told her that he needed to know if she'd miss him, too.

"Leaving you the last time, knowing what you'd given up for us to be a family, I'll never forget that. It was the hardest thing I've ever had to do in my life." She tried her hardest to squeeze the pain away. "And I'm guessing I underestimated how tough it was for you, too. What you lost at the same time." Penny paused, swallowed the thickness in her throat. "I'm sorry if I wasn't there for you. I know that you're not the only one at fault here."

Daniel's hand appeared to be shaking as he reached for his glass. It was something she'd never seen before. Her big, strong husband was unflappable, he always had been. He was tall and broad, his physical stature alone telling other men to back off if they tried to confront him. Nothing could usually rattle him.

But the softness within him, that she could see right now, it scared her more than anything physical could have.

"I'll be honest, Penny. You being sent back overseas when I'd given up my career for us to be a real family, it hurt. I don't think I've ever gotten over that. It was hard, so hard that at the time I didn't know how I was going to pull myself through."

She watched him swallow, like he was fighting an emotion that she'd never seen before. Because he'd always been so strong, and now she could see that he was hurting, too. That maybe he'd been hurting bad all along and she'd been so focused on her own pain of leaving, of being away, that she hadn't recognized it before.

Did he regret what he'd done? What he'd given up for her and for Gabby?

Because she knew, deep within her soul, that she would give up everything in the world for her daughter, to be home. That no matter what the sacrifice, to her it would be worth it.

"I feel like a nobody now. Like I have nothing," he said, the pain leaching into his voice. "I'm a dad, sure, and that's more important than anything, but it's like I no longer have my own identity. I've lost that thing that used to make me *me*."

"You're wrong, Daniel," she whispered, reaching a hand to touch his cheek. She couldn't help it, yearned to touch him so much that she couldn't resist. "You're still that same man."

She knew he was. No matter how angry she was with him, he was a fabulous father. Coming home and seeing that bond between him and Gabby, closer than ever, was all the evidence she needed.

But she still couldn't trust him. Couldn't truly understand what he'd done. No matter how much she could find fault with the way she'd ignored his feelings, or could recognize the cracks that had slowly shattered like a pane of glass within their marriage. She couldn't understand how he'd been pushed far enough to be unfaithful.

He stared into her eyes, not pulling away from her caress.

"You're still the same Daniel I met ten years ago, I promise you are."

"Then why do I feel like I don't know who I am anymore? Like I'm losing everything?"

Penny let her hand drop from his cheek, pushed her plate away for something to do.

"All I know is that I don't want this to end," he said, his voice low and serious. Deep and husky. "You and me, I gave up everything for us and I still would all over again if I had to. For our family. *For our marriage.*"

Penny didn't answer him. Couldn't.

"Penny?" he asked.

She knew what he wanted to know.

"I need time, Daniel." Heavens, did she need time.

His head moved from side to side. "We don't have time, Pen. You fly out in less than five days, and then we won't see each other for months again."

She knew that. Hell, didn't he know that she knew that?

"If we can't survive now, if we can't save our

marriage *now,* then we never will," he said. "I don't know if I can be the husband you deserve anymore, but what I do know is that I'm not scared of trying. If there's one thing you can believe, even if you don't trust me, believe that I'll try. I won't give up, not until you tell me to."

There was an edge of finality to his tone that terrified her. Because she knew it was true.

If she was home for good and Daniel said he was going out with a friend or with his brother, would she believe him any longer? Or would she always worry, have her thoughts betrayed time and again, that he was sneaking off to meet a woman? That he'd hurt her again?

Would she ever be able to look into the eyes of this man sitting before her and trust that it was honesty shining from them? That the words falling from his pillowy lips were honest? Truthful?

"Penny?"

"Don't pressure me, Daniel. Please," she pleaded. "I'm not ready to give you an answer."

The waiter came, cleared the table.

Penny was wondering how she would even stomach the main course, even though she'd been ravenous when they'd first arrived.

"I'm sorry, Penny," he told her. "I'll say it a thousand times if it helps. Because I honestly, truly, hand on my heart mean it." His chocolate-brown eyes bored into hers, filled with more emotion that she could ever believe could be held in a single expression. "I'm so sorry that it's killing me. Even if we can't work through this, even if it is over, I need to know you forgive me."

She looked up at him and took a deep breath.

"I know you're sorry," she said. And she did. She believed him now. "But it doesn't make it any easier for me, okay? One day I'll be able to forgive you, because that's the kind of person I am."

A flicker of hope crossed his face that she moved fast to stamp out. She had no intention of giving him false hope when she had no idea herself what was going to happen.

"What I'm trying to say, Daniel, is that I'll be able to forgive you because you're the father of my child. What I don't know is if I'll ever be able to forgive you as my partner."

Silence stretched so tightly between them it could have snapped.

"Can you honestly tell me that if I'd been unfaithful, if I'd done the same thing to you, that you'd ever be able to move past it? The hurt I feel, the pain…" She held up her hand to stop the conversation. To tell him it was enough. "I just can't give you an answer right now."

It was as if she'd winded him with a fist to his gut, but he regained his composure within half a second.

"Let's enjoy our meal, shall we?"

He gave her a tight smile. She responded by topping up her glass with more red wine.

She wasn't used to drinking, it had been a long time since she'd had anything alcoholic, but tonight she needed it.

To help her make one of the biggest decisions of her life.

It was like he was fighting for his life.

The idea of losing Penny was akin to a life-support machine being taken from a terminal patient. Like a limb being torn from a still-warm body.

But he was tougher than this. Had the will and strength to do *something, anything* to give it his best shot.

To try to survive this.

Hell, he knew tough. He'd been in the depths of hell in the cockpit of a helicopter more times than he could count.

He'd been a helicopter pilot with the navy for almost all his adult life.

Surviving was in his blood.

"Thanks for dinner, Daniel. It was…lovely."

Penny was making an effort and he appreciated it. He'd half expected her to walk off that plane and slap him. To yell and curse and throw him out of the house.

But that wasn't her. She was hurting, and it hurt him to know he was the cause of her pain.

She might be dying a slow, painful death on the inside, but Penny was strong. Women didn't survive to rise through the ranks in the U.S. Army without being intelligent, strong and resourceful.

And Penny was all three.

"Do you want to take a walk before we drive home?"

She looked about to hesitate.

Then surprised him.

"Yeah," she said. "Let's."

Daniel gave the waiter a wave as they left, following Penny down the stairs and into the slightly chilly air outside.

It had been warm when they'd arrived, but the sun was long down and the weather coolish.

"Pen…"

"Daniel…"

They laughed, the second time that night they'd done it.

"Snap," he said.

But he waited for her to go this time, wasn't going to interrupt her.

"I was just going to say that I don't want to fight anymore while I'm here."

He thrust his hands into the pockets of his jeans because he didn't know what else to do with them.

"I don't want to either, Pen."

She wrapped her hands about herself and he had to resist the urge to warm her with his arm. To hold her to him and steal the cold from her body.

"I'm not here long enough for us to waste the time arguing." She sucked in a deep breath. "I don't know if we'll ever work together again as a couple, Daniel, but I'm not going to say no. Because I don't like living with regrets, and I don't want to wish we'd remained civil, that we could have been something great again, but that I was too pig-headed to believe that you were sorry. That I was too self-absorbed to see the problems you were facing."

"Nothing will ever erase what I did, Penny, but I want you to know…"

Penny held up her hand to silence him. He obeyed.

"I need to walk," she said.

Daniel sped up to stay abreast with her fast pace.

"And I need to know the details."

He groaned, like his insides were being turned inside out.

"Penny, no."

She stopped and grabbed his hand, forcing him to spin and stop.

"That wasn't a question, Daniel. I need to know about it. If I don't know, then I can't process it. I can't deal with it. I need to know everything if I'm ever going to understand. I don't want to fight about it. I just want to know."

Despite the cool air a trickle of sweat hit

Daniel's forehead. His hands felt clammy inside his pockets. He pulled them out and ran them down the denim of his jeans instead.

"I don't know if I can do that. I don't, I mean, geez." This was not something he wanted to do. "I can't do that to you, Penny."

She scowled at him before marching off. "You should have thought of that before you screwed someone else." She could have yelled at him, could have screamed, but her words were so quiet and low that it scared him more than any argument could have.

But she was right.

If she wanted to know, then he had to tell her. She deserved that much.

"Okay," he called out, jogging to catch up with her. "Okay," he said, softer this time.

"Don't look at me," she told him, her eyes trained ahead, her pace fast. "Just answer me and don't apologize. Don't pad it out, tell me the details as I ask them."

He nodded, even though she wasn't looking at him and couldn't see the action.

"Where did you meet her?"

This was going to be harder than he thought.

Because not only was this going to hurt Penny like the pierce of a dagger through her heart, it was also like ripping out his own heart again even saying the facts out loud.

Telling her was admitting to himself what he'd done all over again.

"I'd been out with some of the guys who'd just arrived back in," he said, recalling the details of that night. He'd gotten rotten drunk, had felt so low when they were all talking about where they were off to next, what they'd been doing while they were away. He'd felt like such an outsider, when once he'd been at the heart of that team of men. When once he'd been such a part of them that he'd never imagined letting it go. "They all left and I was the last one there. At the bar."

"What was her name?"

No. He wasn't going to go that into detail. "Penny…"

"Her name," she demanded.

"Karen."

"What was so special about—" she hesitated, like she couldn't say her name "—Karen?"

Her voice cut a hole through him, it was so pained.

"I was stupid drunk and we got talking. Sh
was drunk, too." He glanced over at her and sa
the bland expression on her face, like she w
trying to store the facts away somewhere ar
not admit they were true. "She was recently wi
owed, I was lonely and miserable as hell, ar
somehow we ended up at her place. We starte
talking and realized we were each as lonely
the other, and somehow it happened."

"Did you spend the entire night there?"

No. He'd run as soon as he could, in the nice
of ways, because he'd regretted betraying his wi
like that from the moment he'd realized what he
done. The woman hadn't deserved being left li
that, but he hadn't known what else to do. Ha
been too full of guilt and sadness to do anythin
but leave. Not that he was rude to her, they
gotten talking because they were both alone, ar
she'd known he was married.

But the blame was his and his alone. He ha
no intention of letting anyone else shoulder eve
a smidge of it.

"I left soon after. I mean, well…" He didr
know how to explain it. "I didn't want to hurt h
because it wasn't her fault, but I was so disgust

with myself after, for doing what I did just because I was so pathetically desperate to be held and loved by someone, that I left. I swear I've never seen or heard from her again, and I never will. It was the biggest mistake of my life."

Penny turned cold, distant eyes in his direction.

"Leave me, Daniel," she said.

What? "I'm not going to drive off and leave you here alone."

She made a low noise that sounded like a cruel laugh. "Fine. Leave me the keys, then, and you make your own way home. I need to be alone."

He didn't know what to say. Whether to attempt to comfort her. To tell her he was sorry again, to reach for her.

He'd hurt her so bad.

But the look on her face was all soldier. It wasn't his wife standing before him now—the soft, lovable woman he'd married. This was the toughened soldier who could deal with whatever was put in her path. Who made life-or-death decisions and knew how to deal with the consequences.

"Give me the keys, Daniel, or get the hell out

of my way. I need some time and I can't look at you right now."

He didn't hesitate. Daniel reached into his pocket and gave her the keys. She took them, without touching his palm, and turned to walk away. Shoulders straight, hair moving in a wave across her back.

The only difference between his wife right now and the woman who served as a sergeant was the fact she wasn't in uniform and her hair wasn't in the tight braid she preferred when she was working.

It only took a handful of minutes for her to disappear, then he was alone.

Night surrounded him, the voices of other people passing hit him when before it had felt as if he and Penny were the only people in the street.

His wife had walked away from him and he deserved it. Just like she'd deserved the truth, which was why he'd told her.

He hadn't wanted to go back to that night in his mind any more than she had probably wanted to hear it. But it had to come out sometime if they were ever going to move forward.

Maybe now the path would become clearer.

Although from the look on her face before, he seriously doubted it.

# CHAPTER NINE

PENNY wondered if her body was ever going to stop shaking. She felt like a whimpering puppy, unable to stop herself.

So unlike the strong woman she was used to being.

*Karen.*

The name had circled in her mind ever since Daniel had told her. His words falling, crashing through her head. Tumbling over and over like they were never going to stop.

She'd wanted to know and yet she hadn't. But she'd needed to know. The woman within her wanted to know why she'd failed so miserably, what this other woman had had that she didn't. Whether she should blame herself for what had happened, even if it was only in part.

The mother within her wanted to shield herself and those she loved from pain. To push the memories away and try to move forward.

The wife within her was shattered.

But she knew now and she had to deal with it.

Penny pulled up outside their house and sat outside for a few minutes. The lights were on, curtains pulled so she couldn't see in. But she knew the scene she'd find inside.

Daniel's mother would be curled up on the sofa reading a book or watching television, and Gabby would be tucked up in bed, peaceful in sleep.

If she didn't hurry up and get inside, Daniel might even beat her home. She'd driven around aimlessly for ages, thinking, not wanting to go home, because for some reason it didn't truly feel like her home anymore.

Because she no longer felt like she belonged.

Penny hauled herself from the car and headed for the house. She needed to have a nice long sleep, stop fighting the pull of emotions within her, then figure out what the hell she was going to do come morning.

If anything, no matter how hard this night had been, it had told her that Daniel's infidelity was only the tip of a very tall iceberg. Their marriage had been in trouble for longer than she was ready to admit, but instead of acknowledging it, she'd kept a brave smile on her face and acted like everything would turn out okay in the end.

"Penny!"

Vicki's alarmed call rang through the otherwise silent night.

Penny ran. Fast. Her arms pumping at her sides as she sprinted from the driveway and up onto the veranda.

Her feet skidded to a stop, slipping as she grabbed onto the timber railing.

Daniel emerged through the front door, dishevelled, his hair messy like he'd been running his fingers through it over and over again, T-shirt rumpled.

Penny's hand flew to her mouth as her heart starting pounding with fury in her ears.

She couldn't pull her eyes away from Daniel, because his arms carried their daughter.

Gabby lay tucked against him, her head on his chest, tiny like a mouse as his strong hands covered her, held her tight.

"What happened?" Her words were on the verge of a gasp, barely audible.

She didn't have time to ask how Daniel had arrived home before her. Couldn't care less about what they'd discussed. Not now.

Because her daughter, her tiny, precious daughter, was lying limply in his arms like something was seriously wrong.

"Start the car, Penny." Daniel's voice was grim.

Vicki appeared in the doorway behind him. She'd been crying, her eyes were red.

"What happened?" she asked again, unable to move. Penny planted her feet and refused to budge an inch.

"Penny, get in the car!" Daniel ordered, his voice low and full of determination. "I need the soldier right now, okay?"

She nodded, his words snapping logic back into her brain.

She pulled the car keys from her pocket, spun on the spot and took the porch steps two at a time. She had the back door open on the passenger side and the car started before Daniel was even on the sidewalk.

She glanced up to see Vicki still standing where they'd left her, tense worry lines creasing her usually soft face.

Penny pulled back onto the road and looked at Daniel in the rearview mirror. "Where to?"

"The hospital," he said, his voice grim as his eyes met hers, before pulling Gabby closer against him and pressing his lips to her forehead. "She's burning up real bad."

"What happened?" she asked, this time focused on the task at hand. In sergeant mode, rather than helpless mommy.

Ready to do what had to be done.

"Mom was worried about her when she woke up crying, so she let her snuggle up on the couch with her," he said, never taking his eyes or his touch from Gabby. "Then she realized she was hot and clammy, and her temperature skyrocketed."

Penny gripped the wheel tighter, focused on driving. On getting them where they had to go as fast and as safely as possible.

"Why didn't she call us?" She didn't want to put any blame on Vicki though, it wasn't her fault.

She glanced up again and saw that Daniel was watching her now that he had taken his eyes from Gabby. He was staring at her. Like he had something, *a lot even,* to say, but didn't know how to go about it.

"She thought she'd be able to deal with it alone, and she didn't want to interrupt us," he said softly. "She wanted us to enjoy an evening together without having to think about anything else. She called me about twenty minutes ago and I got a taxi here straightaway."

Penny didn't know how to answer that. There was no denying that everyone around them, especially Daniel's family, wanted them to stay together. To work through their problems.

But Gabby was more important than everything else.

If only she hadn't left Daniel to make his own way home!

"Is she…" She didn't know what to ask. What to say. "What are we dealing with here?"

Daniel's voice was its usual deep, strong tone, but there was an undercurrent of worry there that she couldn't help but notice.

"Mom phoned me when she noticed a rash on her chest."

Penny pressed the accelerator more firmly.

"She thought it might be something serious,

like meningococcal. The presence of the rash makes it worse."

Geez.

"Why isn't she awake?" Penny heard the fear in her own voice. She'd forced herself to stay calm and focus on the task at hand, but now...

They should have brought cold soaked towels to help keep the fever down. But then she guessed the most important thing was getting her to where they needed to go without delay.

"She's sleepy because of the fever," he said, his words muffled as he held Gabby tighter, lips against her flushed skin. "I phoned the hospital and they said to get her there as fast as possible because she'd gone downhill so fast. That we would be able to drive faster than we could get an ambulance to collect her."

She flicked her indicator on and pulled into the general hospital entrance.

"I'm sorry, Daniel," she said, emotion choking her voice.

"What are you sorry for?"

She blinked away tears as she parked in the emergency zone.

"For leaving you tonight when we should have been home with Gabby. I should never have…"

Daniel thrust open the door. "You have nothing to be sorry for."

He didn't look back, he just ran.

Penny sniffed back tears as she moved the car out into the main parking area.

If something happened to Gabby, she'd never forgive herself.

Daniel stood, catching his breath, eyes never leaving his little girl.

The doctors had assured him that she would be okay, that she'd been brought there so quickly that they'd be able to run tests and keep a careful eye on her.

But he wasn't so sure.

Daniel looked up when he heard the clack of heels in the corridor behind him. He stepped out, seeing Penny immediately.

"Gabby? Is she…"

Daniel reached out a hand to Penny, to his wife, and let her clutch it tight.

"They don't know what's wrong yet, but they're

going to start trying to cool her down." He pulled Penny gently back into the room with him.

There was a nurse standing beside Gabby, hand on her forehead. She turned to prepare what looked to be ice packs. A fan was blowing nearby.

Machines bleeped, but Daniel had no idea whether they were in the room and attached to his daughter or echoing from somewhere else.

"Daniel…"

*No!*

He pushed past Penny and ran to the bed.

*Please, God, no!*

"Gabby, honey…"

Her tiny body had started to convulse, writhing on the bed.

The nurse stayed calm as he turned what he was sure were wild eyes toward her.

"Do something!" he pleaded. "Please. Please!"

He reached for his little girl, not aware of anything else but the terrifying movement of her body as it continued to convulse.

Hands closed over his arms and tried to drag him back, but he fought it.

"Get off me!"

A blur of white to his right caught his eye, he heard Penny crying, but he wouldn't relinquish his grip on his daughter, holding her so she wouldn't be thrown from the bed.

"Get him out of here!"

The sharpness of a man's direct order pulled Daniel from the void he was lost within.

He looked up, behind him, saw the nurse trying her best to pull him back. Then he saw the doctor as he bent over Gabby, watched as another doctor appeared, rushing forward.

Daniel let himself be pulled away.

"Sorry," he whispered to the nurse whose grip he'd roughly refused. "I'm so sorry."

Penny was beside him then, her hand finding his. The feel of her warm, smooth palm locked against his was comforting, but he couldn't take his eyes from Gabby.

Her tiny body had stopped shaking uncontrollably now and was stripped of clothes. Cold cloths and ice packs covered her.

"Daniel, what's happening? What's wrong with her?"

He shook his head. Shut his eyes to block out

the horror of his daughter on a hospital bed, surrounded by medical staff.

"I don't know." His voice was hoarse, as if he'd been out on the town all night or was emerging from a month of having a cold. "I don't know, Penny."

One of the doctors turned to face them and walked to where they were waiting, near the back of the room.

"Mr. and Mrs. Cartwright?"

Daniel felt Penny start to shake beside him so he dropped her hand and put an arm about her, drawing her close. Trying to be strong for her.

"What's wrong with her?"

The doctor smiled and reached out a hand to touch Penny's other arm. The look on his face calmed Daniel, made him relax the tiniest bit.

"We need to wait for the test results to rule out the worst-case scenarios and try to figure out what's wrong," he said matter-of-factly. "I know that must have been scary for you to watch, but convulsions aren't unusual with high temperatures, and your daughter's temperature certainly peaked."

"But it's coming down now?"

Daniel turned at Penny's question. He held her tighter and she leaned into him for support.

"That's right. We're cooling her down now, her heartbeat is fine, and we need to continue to monitor her carefully."

He cleared his throat and looked the doctor directly in the eye. "What's the worst-case scenario here?"

Daniel didn't look over at Gabby again, couldn't bear to.

The doctor nodded. "Sure. The worst-case scenario, to be honest, would be something like meningococcal, but before you start to worry, I think that would be unlikely."

Daniel felt Penny go limp beside him, from worry or relief he didn't know.

"The presence of a rash does make that within the realm of possibilities, though." The doctor looked over his shoulder and nodded as the other doctor left the room. "Best case? It's a really bad case of the flu, the rash could be coincidental, and it caused a bad fever."

"How likely is that?" Daniel heard himself ask.

"Likely," the doctor insisted. "But given her

age, we're not going to take any risks when it comes to making the correct diagnosis."

Daniel gave the doctor a tight smile and turned his attention back to Penny. She looked as if she was in shock.

"Thanks for being honest with us," he told the doctor. "Is it all right if we stay with her?"

"She'll need to stay overnight, at least until the tests come back. You are both more than welcome to remain with her at all times."

Daniel was numb but he forced the feeling away. He needed to be there for his two girls. No matter how he was feeling or what he was thinking.

He was a father and a husband, and that meant he had to put his family first.

"Penny?"

Her eyes looked drained, empty, when she turned to face him. Her skin pale, lacking its usual golden glow.

The doctor left them, the nurse still hovering over Gabby.

His wife turned her grief-stricken face toward him, reached one hand up to place it on his shoulder as she leaned into him for a hug.

Daniel held her, too, wrapped both his arms around her and squeezed her against him, lips pressed to her hair, bodies pressed hard into one another's.

He relaxed into Penny as she held on to him like she'd never let go. Like nothing had torn them apart and they hadn't been estranged, forced apart by distance and emotion, these past few months.

All the fighting, the pain, the heartache of what had happened fell away.

Until they were just two people who needed one another.

Two people who never wanted to let go of the other.

Penny sobbed gently in his arms, snuffling into his chest, her face tucked against him. He released one of his hands from her waist and touched the back of her hair, let his fingers work through the softness of each silky dark strand.

She tilted her head back then, tipped her tear-stained face up to him, eyes wide, worry and sadness like pools within them.

"I'm so sorry, Penny. I'm..."

She shook her head and made him stop. The tilt

of her head telling him no. That she didn't want him to talk.

Penny stood on tiptoe, her petite frame reaching up toward him.

Daniel didn't move. Didn't breathe. Was paralyzed and unable to do a thing.

She brought her lips slowly, painfully slowly, toward his. He felt her breath whisper across his lips before her mouth touched his.

Penny moved her lips tenderly, her hand moving to hover across his cheek as she did so.

Their mouths met for only a moment, but it filled Daniel with hope. A hope that had been missing within him, but once ignited was like the steady beat of a drum, a light that had been dull and was now shining bright.

"Thank you," she whispered.

He was numb as she stepped away, hand still touching his cheek.

Daniel raised an eyebrow. "For what?" he mumbled.

"For being such a great dad," she said, quietly so they couldn't be overheard. "There's no one else in the world I would have trusted to leave our daughter with while I was away. You're a wonderful father, and I don't think I've ever told you that before."

Daniel shook his head, but Penny only stepped back and pressed a finger to her lips.

"There are so many things I never told you, and I'm sorry. You gave up so much to be a great dad, and I'm proud of you."

Daniel felt like a child who'd finally been given a gold star in class. A warmth spread through him, warming him when before he'd been chilled.

"And the answer is yes."

"Yes?" he repeated.

She let her head move up and down in a nod. "You asked me to give you a chance. To let you prove yourself to me. And the answer is yes," Penny told him. "I don't know if we can ever be a couple again, Daniel, but I'm not saying no."

He reached for her again, slung his arm around her shoulder as they both turned toward Gabby.

"She's the most important thing in the world, Penny."

She tucked her head against his shoulder. "She's going to be okay, I just know it."

They stood together and looked at their little

girl, and Daniel felt a pain in his chest that threatened to stop his heart.

He had no idea how it was possible to feel such a strong pull of emotions. Having Penny by his side, feeling her body touch his when they'd spent so long with a void between them, gave him a strength he couldn't define.

But seeing Gabby on a hospital bed, when the last time he'd set foot within a hospital was the day she'd been born, sent a shiver down his spine that threatened to chill every pore of his skin.

"Do you remember the last time we were here?"

Daniel chuckled, reaching for Penny's hand again.

"You read my mind. I was just remembering the night we rushed in here," he said.

"I was so scared," Penny told him, her eyes never leaving the bed their daughter lay upon. "It all happened so fast, and the next thing I knew we were holding Gabby."

Daniel looked up at the overhead lights to blink away a row of tears as they filled his eyes.

"No matter what happens, Penny, we made the most beautiful little girl."

Penny swiveled to look at him before moving

away a step and sinking into one of the chairs beside the bed.

She reached out to hold Gabby's hand—a hand that looked so tiny tonight he hardly recognized it.

Daniel sat down in the chair beside her.

"She's going to be fine, Pen."

"I know," she replied. "But I'm just so glad that we're both here beside her."

When she met his gaze, when her soft brown eyes hit his, a warmth spread through him.

Because it was the first time in what felt like forever that he thought they might have a chance of being what they'd once been.

Best friends. Lovers.

Life partners.

# CHAPTER TEN

PENNY woke up with a dry mouth and her head resting on something that was somehow familiar.

She stretched her legs out and raised her head. *Oh.*

"Hey."

A warm flush spread across her cheeks and down her neck.

It had been a long time since she'd woken up beside Daniel like this, felt his eyes trawl hers, watched the soft dimple crease at the side of his mouth as he spoke.

"Morning," she croaked.

It took her a second to realize where she was. Why they were sitting side by side, in the early morning, rather than with their heads on pillows.

Then it all came crashing back to her.

"Gabby?" Her voice was even weaker this time.

Daniel's smile hit his eyes. "She's fine."

"How long have I been sleeping?" She should

have been holding Gabby's hand all night, waiting for her to wake up. Instead of falling asleep and leaving her alone.

"It's okay," Daniel told her, skimming the side of her face with one outstretched finger before standing. "She's just nodded off again, but she's been talking."

He must have seen the question mark on her face.

"Talking and eating," he added.

Penny took the hand Daniel held out and pulled herself up to her feet.

"I should never have…"

"You needed the sleep," he said. "Don't beat yourself up about getting some shut-eye. You've flown halfway around the world, not to mention spending the last however many months serving. I think you deserve a little sleep in with that kind of jet lag."

"Daddy?"

Gabby's tiny voice put a stop to their conversation. They both shuffled almost instantly to her side, but Penny held back. She'd asked for her father, and there was only room for one of them to hold her hand.

She stole her eyes away from Gabby to glance at Daniel, saw the pained yet happy expression on his face as he bent to kiss their daughter on her forehead.

But it was the bright eyes and excited words that put Penny's heart in her mouth.

"Mommy!" Gabby gasped the word, her eyes so wide they looked ready to pop.

She jumped forward, nearly pushing Daniel out of the way in her hurry to touch Gabby. So pleased to be wanted, to hear the excitement in her daughter's voice.

"Hey, baby," she said, covering Gabby's hand and squeezing it. "You gave us such a fright."

Gabby didn't say anything, but she never dropped her eyes, didn't so much as blink. Like she was so happy to have her mother beside her, holding her hand, that she didn't want to look away and find she'd disappeared.

Penny felt the same.

"What happened?" Gabby asked.

Daniel walked around to the other side of the bed, sinking down onto the edge of it to give her a cuddle.

"Well…"

"Good morning!" The doctor's cheery voice made them all look up.

"Morning," Penny and Daniel both replied without looking up.

"I see our patient is wide-awake," he said, smiling at Gabby before lifting the chart from the end of her bed. When he placed it back down, he folded his arms and looked between them.

"The good news is that Gabby doesn't have anything serious."

"It's not meningococcal?" Penny asked.

The doctor shook his head. "Thankfully we've been able to rule that out. It appears she just has a very bad strain of the flu, hence the high temperature. I'm happy to discharge her so long as she has a close eye kept on her. Any sign of a fever again or anything else out of the ordinary, and I want her straight back here. But she should be fine within twenty-four hours."

"Yes, sir," said Penny, smiling as she gave him a mock salute.

"Ah, of course. I heard from the nurse that you were a soldier," the doctor told her.

"United States Army Sergeant," Penny responded, left hand still covering her daughter's.

"I take it you're home for good now?"

Didn't she wish. Penny cleared her throat and avoided looking at Daniel. Or Gabby. It was hard enough dealing with her own emotions without seeing the looks on their faces.

"Unfortunately, no. I'm here on short-term leave, back with my unit next week, before I return home for good."

The doctor didn't react either way, just gave her a warm smile and a nod before turning to leave.

"Take care, then, soldier. God bless."

Penny still avoided Daniel as she turned around, wishing she hadn't had to be reminded of what she was so shortly about to leave behind. Again.

"Let's get you home, miss."

Gabby grinned and rubbed her tiny thumb over Penny's hand.

"I'll bring the car around the front," Daniel told them, dropping a kiss to Gabby's forehead.

Penny returned his smile even though her heart was breaking all over again. She had no idea how she was going to board that plane next week.

It was going to be the hardest thing she'd ever done.

She'd thrown grenades and completed some of

the hardest combat training courses in the world. But nothing, *nothing,* compared to this.

All she could think about was leaving Gabby all over again, just when they'd started to connect again. Her daughter's face lighting up at seeing her today, calling for her when she already had her beloved father beside her, it made her feel alive. Like she hadn't been herself and she was slowly recovering from whatever had been holding her captive until now.

And Daniel. She shut her eyes for a moment. Daniel was…still her husband. And she didn't know what was going to happen there, or what *could* happen there. Whether they could ever go back to the way things used to be.

She had such limited time to act, to decide what to do and to figure out how she was going to cope.

What she had to do was draw on the strength of knowing that soon, she *would* be coming home for good.

She just had to decide now what it was she'd be coming home to next time.

Gabby was settled in her room like a princess, snuggled up watching a DVD. They'd moved the television from the master bedroom onto her dresser, and she couldn't have been happier. After a day running around looking after her, Penny was exhausted. But at least Gabby was feeling better, was starting to get her appetite back.

"I guess we'll be having a quiet night in?" Daniel asked.

Penny kept stirring the pasta sauce, leaning over the large pot to inhale the tomato infused with fresh basil.

"As opposed to?"

Daniel came up behind her and reached for the spoon, plucking it from her hand.

"I have a few things I want to do with you, while you're back. If you're still up to giving me a chance, that is?"

*Oh.*

She watched as he tasted the sauce off the spoon, her eyes tracing his mouth as he did so.

"Perfect."

She grabbed the wooden spoon before he could drop it back into the pot.

"No."

"No?" he repeated.

She tried to focus on manners instead of the cheeky, irresistible-as-hell look on his face.

"You don't put a spoon back in there after licking it!"

He shrugged, dimple creasing at the corner of his mouth as he did so. "We're all family. What does it matter?"

"What does it matter?" Penny rolled her eyes and opened the drawer to find another spoon. "It's not good hygiene."

Daniel laughed. He actually opened his mouth wide and laughed at her. "Okay, I won't do it again." He paused, tilted his head while he was looking at her. "I think you've spent too long in the army and not enough time observing the disgusting things children, your daughter in particular, can do with food."

Huh. "I guess if she's learning her manners from you she gets up to all sorts of disgusting things."

Penny tried to sound serious but she didn't really care. What she liked was the easy banter between them. Play-arguing like they used to. Chatting and laughing for the sake of it.

"You know, when you think about it, we haven't

actually spent that much time together. Well, in the past few years anyway."

Daniel arched an eyebrow in her direction as he leaned back against the counter on the other side of the kitchen. "Meaning?"

She finished stirring and filled another large saucepan with water for the pasta. "I just mean that in ten years together we've probably only spent maybe a third of that time *actually together*."

He moved his head from side to side like he was thinking about it, or maybe agreeing with her. She couldn't tell.

"I guess you're right."

"Think about it," she said. "We had one year together before we went off to the army and navy, add our terms overseas in there, and we've been more absent than together."

His eyes met hers. "Maybe that's why this has been so hard."

Tears blurred her vision and she turned back to the almost boiling water. "It's like we always had this idea of what it would be like when we both moved back here for good, but we didn't really know what it was going to be like."

Daniel didn't say anything. As if he wasn't sure how to broach the subject, how to contribute to the conversation, without hurting her.

"I don't want you to think I'm making excuses, Pen, or that I want to bring this up again, but thinking you were coming home then having that snatched away from me..." He ran a hand through his thick, dark hair and tugged on the end of it. "It was like we had this fantasy of what it was going to be like one day, like it would make everything right, and when that day came it wasn't as I'd imagined it to be."

She kept her back turned. "What if it had worked out? What if we'd both finished up at the same time like we'd planned? Been together?"

She heard him sigh behind her.

"Honestly? I don't know for sure, but maybe it wouldn't have been so easy. Adjusting to being home full-time is hard, Penny. No matter how much you think you want to come home, you're going to miss the army so bad you'll feel like a crack addict trying to go cold turkey. We've both made out like everything's been okay all this time, because that's the kind of people we are, but there are times when it's been truly hard."

As much as she wanted to deny it, to not believe him, she had a feeling he was right. Because no matter how badly she wanted to come home, to be a full-time mommy and leave her career behind, leaving was going to be tough. Just like being a proper wife again would have been tough, even if Daniel hadn't been unfaithful.

Knowing that she was giving that life away forever was not an easy decision. It was one they'd both been prepared to make, a sacrifice they'd both chosen, but it wasn't easy. But she'd only ever joined the army as a way to finish her degree, for the scholarship. She'd never intended on serving more than the mandatory four years of service.

Penny dropped the pasta into the pot as the water started to bubble and blinked away her tears. This was not the time to be getting all emotional. She had a daughter down the hall to care for, less than four days to enjoy her company and a husband standing behind her who was trying so hard she was starting to think that maybe he did truly deserve that second chance he was asking for.

"So what was it you said you had planned?" she

asked, turning a happy face toward him when she spun around.

Daniel was still standing on the other side of the kitchen, leaning against the counter, but the way he was watching her made it feel like he was standing less than a foot away. She couldn't tear her eyes from his stubble-grazed chin, the soft curve of his mouth, the endless brown pools of his eyes… Hell!

He looked…hungry. Was watching her in a way that sent an involuntary shiver down her spine and a tingle through her lower legs.

"I want it to be a surprise," he told her.

She hated surprises. "I don't know, Daniel. I'm not sure about anything that involves leaving Gabby, to be honest."

He shook his head.

"How about a compromise," he suggested. "We'll spend as much time as a family as we can, but when Gabby goes to bed at night, then we can spend time together. The two of us."

Even if she was going to let him prove himself to her, being alone with him, spending intimate time together, made her feel like a schoolgirl about to go on a first date with her dream crush.

"That's what we did last time, Daniel, and look what happened."

He shook his head.

"I'm as worried about her as you are, Penny, but us spending time together is important, too."

She sighed, knowing in her heart that what he said was true. The last thing she wanted was to leave Gabby after what had happened, but she couldn't blame her mother-in-law for the way things had turned out last night. It could have happened to any of them. And in less than a week, she wouldn't have the luxury of deciding to stay home. Would have to go back to trusting Daniel and Vicki to care for Gabby in her absence.

"Give me a chance, Penny, please." Daniel took her hand and stared straight into her eyes. "Let me show you why I think we can find a way to make this work."

"I've already told you I will," she said softly.

He tucked a finger under her chin and tilted her face. There was still distance between them, a distance she wanted to close and yet didn't. Because even the thought of letting him in again still terrified her.

"Then show me," he said, voice low and tender as he captivated her with his gaze. "I don't need to tell you how few days we have left."

Penny looked down, couldn't face talking about how little time she had left here.

"Don't remind me, Daniel," she pleaded. "Please don't."

He curled his fingers tighter for a moment, then trailed them slowly down her neck and away.

"Let me in, Penny. If we don't spend time together, if you don't put your words into action, we'll never know what could have been. This is the time we need to be honest with each other about how we're feeling, to see if we can fix *us*."

He was right, she knew that. There was no point telling him one thing but being too scared to follow through. If she was truly going to give Daniel a chance.... Her heart thumped overtime, made her mouth dry as she tried to think what to say to him.

"How about tomorrow night?" she croaked.

Daniel's smile lit his entire face. "Tomorrow night," he repeated.

She turned back to the pasta sauce, nervously stirring it, unsure what else to do.

"We're almost ready here," she told him.

She could sense Daniel behind her but he didn't touch her. Penny was relieved. Her feelings, emotions, were all over the place. She didn't know what she wanted, what she thought, what she should do.

"Should we eat dinner in Gabby's room with her?"

"That'd be great."

Daniel shuffled behind her and Penny held her breath. It was like her body was on high alert, mind thrumming with energy and worried thoughts, waiting for his touch. For his words.

For his anything.

"I'll go tell her and set up while you serve."

"Sure."

Penny waited until his feet echoed on the timber floor before she pivoted to steal a glance at him as he walked away.

Daniel had always appealed to her physically, from the first time she'd ever set eyes upon him. His thick, dark hair that begged for fingers to be run through it, the breadth of his shoulders and biceps, muscled and strong from all the years he'd spent training with the navy.

From behind, he looked big. But had she been standing in front of him, she'd have seen how his physique was balanced by a softness that had always appealed to her. He could protect her if ever she needed it, but his eyes had a kindness, an openness that showed how gentle he was inside.

Penny turned back to her sauce as he disappeared down the hall and flicked the gas hob off. She reached for the bowls to start serving dinner, trying to distract herself but unable to.

She'd tried so hard to push him away. Had had every right to want to end things, to not even attempt to forgive him.

But in her heart she wanted to give him a chance. A real chance. No matter how hard or impossible that might seem now.

This was never going to get any easier. She could either block him out and keep her heart locked away to stop it from being hurt again. Or she could put her feelings and emotions on the line, open up and face hurt again, to see if she could ever trust and love Daniel.

It was what she wanted, what she wished she could do, but she couldn't stop the worry, the terror trembling through her body at the thought of following through with her thoughts and hopes.

Because that would mean working through something she had no idea how she'd ever forget. Letting Daniel touch her, really touch her again. Letting him in both physically and emotionally.

And no matter how much she wanted to, it was going to be the hardest thing she'd ever tried to do.

"You need any help?" Daniel called out to her.

Penny put the spoons down, took a deep breath and called back to him.

"Yeah, that'd be great."

She started spooning sauce over the spaghetti.

If she didn't let him in now, actually give him a chance to prove himself, she was going to run out of time.

Daniel stood beside the bed before settling down on Gabby's chair. The action itself set her off into hysterical giggles.

"Daddy! That's way too small for you."

He fidgeted until he made her small wooden chair creak, like a giant in a fairy's seat.

"Daddy!"

He started to slurp his pasta, trying hard not to laugh as he ignored Gabby's protests at his behavior.

"Daddy!"

Penny joined in, sitting cross-legged on Gabby's bed.

"Daniel, be careful," she scolded.

He shrugged dramatically, finishing his mouthful. "What?"

Gabby bounced so hard she splashed sauce on the bed.

"You're too heavy! You'll break it."

He put down his fork and grinned at her. "I promise I won't, honey."

She huffed. "You will."

He glanced at Penny and saw the smile on her face. She'd looked happy while she was here, especially at Gabby's party, but this was the first time he'd seen her so relaxed. The kind of relaxed they'd always used to be around one another.

"Sweetheart, I was only playing around."

Gabby still looked worried. "Come up on the bed and sit with us."

There wasn't much room but he wasn't going to say no.

"This is fun," said Gabby, as he climbed on. "I feel way better now, you know."

Daniel was listening to his daughter, but his eyes were on Penny. Her expression hadn't changed, she was still relaxed, comfortable looking, even though he was now cross-legged beside her, knee touching hers.

She picked up her fork again and started to twirl her spaghetti. Gabby was happily doing the same.

But it was Penny who he couldn't take his eyes off, and she returned his gaze. Even though her flushed cheeks signaled a hint of embarrassment, she only glanced away to bring the pasta to her mouth, before turning her eyes back to his again.

"What are we going to do tomorrow?" he asked.

Penny didn't respond. Gabby practically started to bounce again. Clearly over the worst of her flu.

"What about work?"

"It's the weekend," he told her. "And stop bouncing, you'll make yourself sick."

"But you sometimes work on a Saturday," Gabby said, ignoring him.

Daniel shook his head and pushed his knee a little firmer against Penny's.

"Not tomorrow, kid. Tomorrow we spend the entire day together."

Penny reached out an arm and put it around Gabby.

"And then tomorrow night, we thought we'd ask your grandma over again."

"We did?" Daniel raised an eyebrow as he asked.

"Yeah," Penny said, throwing him a smile as she kissed Gabby on the head.

"Of course." Daniel shook his head as he realized that was her way of telling him she'd decided to agree to his date suggestion. "Because tomorrow night I'm taking your mom out dancing."

"Dancing?" Penny and Gabby said the word at exactly the same time, only Penny sounded terrified and Gabby looked beside herself with excitement.

"Yes, dancing," he repeated, before turning his gaze to Penny and giving her a wink. "And we're going to have a great time."

They hadn't been out on the town since before they were married, but tomorrow night he was going to make sure they had a great time. Like they used to have.

"I didn't even know you could dance, Daddy," Gabby said.

Penny laughed and he tried to frown and failed miserably, cheeks burning from trying so hard not to smile.

"It's your mom who can dance," he told Gabby. "She's the best dancer I've ever seen. Me? I just shuffle along beside her."

Penny hugged Gabby tighter as Daniel watched her, but she didn't argue. The playful twinkle in her eyes was all he needed as encouragement.

For the first time in a long while, it was like a cloud of happiness was shining over him, rather than a gray cloud of gloom.

# CHAPTER ELEVEN

PENNY stretched her limbs and kept her eyes firmly shut. It seemed like forever since she'd been able to lie in bed without waking at the crack of dawn.

She raised her head and squinted at the bedside clock.

Who was she kidding. It *had* been forever since she'd been able to do this.

Only the last thing she wanted to be doing today, with so few days left here, was lounging about in bed. No matter how good it felt.

She didn't need to look to her right to see if Daniel was still beside her. He was heavy enough to weigh his side of the bed down and she would have known if he was there. Even though they didn't touch in the night, she always knew he was there. Knew that his body was beside hers.

Penny forced her legs from the bed and straightened her pajamas. Voices wafted down to her and she followed them.

She was tempted to pause in the hall and listen, but she didn't want to sneak up on them. Gabby was yapping away to Daniel, and he was hardly getting a word in. Not that he'd care.

Penny peeked into the bathroom to find Daniel leaning over the hand basin shaving, with Gabby standing on a stool beside him.

She put her hand over her mouth to stop from laughing. So they didn't know she was standing in the doorway.

Gabby's face was reflected in the mirror, covered in Daniel's white shaving cream. She was using a toothbrush to scrape the cream off, copying her father.

She'd never seen anything so beautiful in her life.

No matter what happened between her and Daniel, she couldn't ask for a better father for their daughter. He'd royally stuffed up as a husband, but as a dad? He couldn't be faulted.

And she was starting to realize that maybe, just maybe, Daniel couldn't shoulder all the blame for their marriage falling apart.

"Hey, you." Daniel had a towel tucked around his waist, torso bare from his shower. "I didn't want to wake you so I used this bathroom."

"Thanks for letting me sleep in."

Gabby patted more shaving cream onto her cheeks. "Do you want to see me shave, Mommy?"

Penny did her best to keep her mouth in a straight line. "Sure." She averted her gaze from Daniel, knowing they'd both crack up if they made eye contact.

"I'm going to shave just like Daddy when I grow up."

This time she did look at Daniel and they laughed.

"What?" Gabby asked, all open-mouthed and innocent-eyed.

Penny tried to avert her gaze from Daniel's and ended up with her eyes trailing dangerously over his torso. Down the tiny smattering of hair that spiked down low, golden skin so taut and soft…

*Oh.*

She looked up to see he was watching her back, that he'd seen exactly what she was looking at. Would be able to tell what she was thinking.

Gabby was still busily swiping at her face with

her toothbrush and rinsing it off just like Daniel had been with his razor.

But there was a heat in the room now that had nothing to do with the hot tap being run.

And it terrified her.

Because she was so worried about being intimate with Daniel again, after so long and after what had happened, and yet her body was rebelling with a mind all its own.

Knowing he was in bed beside her was one thing, but touching him again? Actually being husband and wife again in the truest sense? That was what scared her.

"Mommy? Are you okay?"

She backed up a couple steps. "Oh, it's nothing, honey. I'm just so pleased I'm here to see you do things like shave with your dad in the morning."

Gabby grinned and went back to playing at the basin.

Daniel tightened the towel around his waist like he didn't know what else to do.

"How about we head out for breakfast somewhere?"

Penny was pleased to have an excuse to escape. "Sounds good."

"For pancakes?" Gabby piped up.

"Sure, kiddo," Daniel said. But his eyes never left Penny's, made her feel like there was no one else in the world except for her. That she was so special to him that he didn't care what else went on around them.

It was a feeling she hadn't experienced in a long while. A warm, settling sensation that she'd missed so bad it had been like a mother being torn from her child forever.

"I'll go get ready," Penny told them.

Daniel was still watching her, but Gabby was otherwise occupied.

Penny fled down the hall like someone had lit the back of her pajamas alight.

Running scared, but at the same time ready to run back into the fire to risk being burned.

A hand caught her arm, stopped her from taking another step. Forced her to stop moving.

"Penny."

She stopped. Caught. Knowing he was too close. Not wanting him half-naked behind her.

"I know it's going to be hard going back." His voice was husky, full of meaning. "But if we can make it work it'll be worth it."

She nodded, head moving in a slow arc up and down. He was right. He was so right, she knew it because of the flutter in her chest, the heat tickling across every inch of her skin.

"We made a life together, Penny."

They were the words that made her turn. That made her breath catch in her throat in a gasp.

"See that little girl in there? *She's ours.* No one can ever take that away from us."

She tipped back, the smallest motion of her body, but it was enough to touch Daniel, to allow his mouth to touch her hair, to allow her back to skim his chest.

Penny tilted her head to the side and looked back at Gabby. Saw her smiling at herself in the mirror as she continued to play, even with her father no longer by her side.

"If we hadn't met, we wouldn't have her. We wouldn't have had all those years of being happy together. All those memories of having fun, of being in love."

"I know," she whispered, not wanting Gabby to hear them.

Daniel sighed into her hair, touched both his hands to her forearms, held her in place. She was clothed but it was such a firm, intimate touch that it made her feel as if they were both naked. As if there was nothing else to think about other than their skin colliding, than his warm breath on the back of her neck.

"I don't want to bring this up again, Pen, I don't, but…"

She waited. Not wanting to go there again either but knowing they were still so far from putting it behind them. She wanted so badly to say *Then don't.*

"We can't throw away something so special for something that was so meaningless."

Her back bristled and he knew it. Caught the moment as it struck, before it was too late to be saved.

"I know it sounds clichéd and pathetic, but it *was* meaningless. Compared to what we had, to what we could still have…" He stayed still, hands firm against her. "There is nothing more important to me than you and Gabby, and you need to believe that."

Penny knew what he was trying to say and she was tired of calling him out on it. Was sick of blaming him, of holding anger and sadness in her heart when she didn't have space to feel down. She'd already failed to listen to him once, and it wasn't a mistake she wanted to make again.

"I don't blame you anymore," she told him, stepping away from him. Needing to distance herself physically. "I'm still angry, but I don't blame you, Daniel. Not now."

He didn't say anything. Probably had no idea *what* to say.

"I'll be ready soon," she said, her voice louder this time so Gabby could hear if she was listening.

Penny knew Daniel was watching her. A hot flush hit her cheeks as she walked away, because she knew he was probably checking her out. Was as aroused as she was from being so close to one another yet so unable to do anything about it.

She needed to get out of the house.

Breakfast was going to be a good distraction, but their date tonight?

The thought of dancing with Daniel had her stomach leaping like snakes had taken possession of it. After feeling him behind her, touching him, being so close she could almost taste him...

it was too much for her to resist if the temptation presented itself. And it would.

Maybe going on a date with her husband wasn't such a smart move.

Unless she was actually ready to see if they could still be the Danny and Pen of old again.

Just like old times.

Penny groaned as she peeled off her clothes and jumped in the shower.

Being married wasn't supposed to be this hard.

And being on the verge of happy wasn't supposed to feel so traitorous.

If she did let Daniel back in again, forgave him for his mistake and tried her hardest to move forward, *to forget,* would that mean she'd compromised on her principles? Mean that she thought it was okay for a husband to be unfaithful?

Or would it mean that she was big enough to forgive for a sin she'd always thought was the worst a partner could make? That she was a better, more open, loving person than she'd ever thought she could be in a situation that had almost broken her heart into more pieces than a jigsaw puzzle?

Penny let the water run over her face, eyes shut to the bliss of the shower.

Whatever happened, she was ready to forgive herself.

*Finally.*

And it was herself she needed to forgive in order to move on.

If her heart told her to make room for her husband again, then she was prepared to accept it.

The thought alone made her chest start to pound, made it sound as if the sea was roaring in her ears.

Being in Daniel's arms again would be like finding a long-lost love, one who it felt like she'd been pining for all her life.

She needed to forgive herself, stop shouldering the blame for what had happened, for abandoning her husband, and give herself the opportunity to embrace the future.

"They were the best pancakes ever."

Daniel watched as Penny dipped her head to rest on top of Gabby's. She rubbed Gabby's belly and laughed.

"How do you fit so much in there?"

Gabby shrugged. "I don't know. Sometimes I think I might pop."

Daniel slung his arm across the back of the booth seat, his other arm raised to bring the coffee cup to his lips. Strong, black coffee that took the edge of the too-little sleep he'd had last night.

He'd lain awake for hours. Thinking. Trying to figure out what he could do, what he'd do if nothing worked out as he hoped it would.

He'd already lost so much this year. His friends that he saw everyday, the workmates he thought of as extended family—they'd been eliminated from his daily life as if he'd never see them again. The fact that he'd only signed up for an eight-year term didn't make walking away any easier. Not after almost a decade of serving with the same guys.

So the thought of losing this happy little family scene…it was more painful than he could ever find words to describe. It would always have hurt losing Penny. No matter when it happened, it would take a part of him that could never heal or regenerate.

There was nothing in the world he'd say no

to, nothing he wouldn't sacrifice for either of his girls.

Moments like this were worth anything he had to give.

"Any more pancakes here?"

Gabby groaned and rubbed at her belly. "No," she said, knowing the question was directed at her.

The waitress laughed and took their plates. "I told you two would be plenty, didn't I?"

Gabby giggled and leaned deeper against her mom.

"We'll grab the check, thanks." Daniel smiled up to the waitress before bringing his attention back to his family.

"What's on the agenda for the rest of the day?"

"We could go see Uncle Tommy," suggested Gabby.

Daniel resisted the urge to laugh. She had tiny smears of maple syrup tickling against the edges of her mouth.

"We could, or maybe we could all go see a movie together?"

The look in Penny's eyes told him it was a good suggestion.

"Like a family movie day?" Gabby asked.

"Yeah, just like that," he replied.

"I think that sounds like a great idea, but maybe we should take a walk first. I'll never fit back into my work clothes if I keep eating like this while I'm home."

Gabby laughed. Daniel tried to join in, but it didn't come naturally. Every mention, every thought about Penny going back, leaving them again, made sadness beat through his body.

Knowing that it'd be months before they could sit like this again.

Knowing the risks of her going back overseas with her unit.

"Mommy, what do you wear to work?"

Gabby's question was innocent enough, but Daniel could see it had put Penny on high alert. No matter how much she tried to hide it.

"You know what? When I come home next, I'll wear my work clothes off the plane. That way you can see them."

Gabby raised her eyebrows. "Are they secret clothes?"

Daniel found himself holding his breath while Penny sighed in response.

"Not secret, darling, just different, that's all," Penny told her. "When I'm home for good, I'll tell you all about the clothes I wear and the work I did, okay?"

Gabby looked as if she'd lost interest, but Daniel hadn't. He knew why Penny wanted to shield their daughter from the work she did, but he also knew how much pleasure Gabby would have, one day, in hearing about the work her mother had done. What she'd been involved in.

"How about once Mommy's back for good, we tell you stories about all the work we both did?" Daniel suggested, gazing at Penny. He could see from the way she was watching him that she knew what he meant. That he wanted to sit down as a family, *together,* and talk about the way they'd both served their countries. "We've both got some pretty good stories about what we've been up to."

Gabby shrugged, looking happy but not caring, her attention diverted. She was busy looking around the restaurant now, ready to go and move on to the next thing.

But Penny cared.

"I'd like that," she said, voice barely more than a whisper.

He nodded, but her words meant so much to him.

"I'm proud of everything you've done, Pen," he told her honestly. "Even if it's made things hard on us, I'm so proud of your work. Of what you've been able to achieve."

She looked down, eyelashes shielding her eyes, not letting him see the expression there.

"I'm proud of you, too. I am," Penny said.

"Mommy, what's wrong?"

Gabby's attention had strayed and was back to them again, and her tiny hand was rubbing at her mom's arm.

"Sweetheart, I'm fine," Penny said, eyes full of bravery now. "It's sad thinking about leaving you again, that's all, and I can't wait to be home for good."

Gabby snuggled into her and Daniel stood up, went to pay the bill to give them a moment alone.

The thing was, he didn't want to give them even a second alone. He wanted to be with them both all the time.

But for now, he had to feel fortunate that Penny

was back in his life at all, however fleetingly it might be. And hope that next time, it was him she was coming back to.

To their home, their daughter, their lives together.

It wasn't going to be easy. But then nothing worth fighting for ever was.

"Grandma's here!" Gabby's high-pitched voice almost deafened Daniel.

It was like a repeat of the night he'd taken Penny out for dinner, only he hoped the ending turned out to be completely the opposite.

"Penny?" he called.

"Coming!"

Gabby spun around from the window, eyes alight.

"I'm going to see what she's wearing."

He couldn't help but laugh as she took off to find her mom. "Don't worry about letting your grandma in, then."

She either didn't hear him or didn't care. Daniel went to let his mother in himself, then frowned as he saw that Tom was with her.

"Geez, don't you have anything better to do on a Saturday night?" he asked his brother.

Tom glowered at him. "No, *actually,*" he said sarcastically. "I've just had notice that I'm shipping out in a few days and I thought I'd spend some time with my niece."

Daniel wished he hadn't snapped.

"Enough of the bickering, you two. Come on."

His mother emerged, cake tin in her hands as she bustled past.

"How you doing, winning your wife back?"

Now Daniel was angry. "Seriously, Tom, just when I was about to apologize for being rude."

His brother gave him a slap on the back as he passed. "I'm still pissed at you for what you did, can't let you off that easy."

Daniel glared at him, his pulse ticking rapidly in his neck.

"Sorry." Tom put his hands up in the air. "I'll be more sensitive next time. And for what it's worth, I *do* hope she takes you back. This family is better for having Penny in it, and I want you guys to be happy."

"Who do you want to be happy?"

Daniel looked up at the same time as Tom did.

*Geez.*

If he'd thought she'd looked good the other night, tonight she looked incredible.

Amazing.

Her dress was shorter than he'd seen her wear in years, but then it had been years since they'd had a night out on the town together, too.

"Wow!" Tom beat Daniel to the punch before he was even able to form words of his own. "You look fantastic, Pen."

"Thanks." Her voice was low, shy, but she let Tom kiss her on the cheek.

"You're going to have a great night out."

"What are you doing here anyway?" Penny asked.

Tom raised his shoulders then let them fall. "Thought I'd hang out with Mom and my favorite niece for a bit."

"I'm your *only* niece, Uncle Tom," said Gabby, sidling up to him and wrapping her hands around his leg, tugging him into the living room.

Daniel found his tongue, managed to make his body work again as Tom started to walk backwards, laughing at Gabby.

"You do look incredible, Penny," Daniel told

her, pleased that Tom had stepped away, even if he had given her a rogue wink before disappearing from sight.

"Really? I hope it's not too much." She fingered the edge of her dress as she stood there, nervous.

"It's not too much. You look stunning." He couldn't have said more honest words if he'd tried. She was so beautiful it stole his breath away.

There was a toot of a car horn outside.

"Shall we go?"

Penny touched his hand as he reached for her, let her fingers brush his. "Let me grab my purse and say goodbye to Gabby."

He reached for her wrist and caught it. Paused before tugging her gently toward him.

Daniel caught the faintest hint of her perfume, fought not to shut his eyes against the softness of her body against him.

"Thank you," he said, lips achingly close to her mouth as he spoke.

"For what?" She didn't meet his gaze, kept her eyes lowered, giving him only her dark lashes to focus on again.

"For giving me a second chance."

They stood, facing one another, so close, not moving. Their breathing synchronized, Daniel's heart beating fast.

There was nothing left to say.

The test would be in whether they could fall in love and stay in love again. Whether they could both move on, forgive and forget.

Because even though Penny had found this hard, he had, too. He'd behaved in a way he'd never thought he was capable of. Had hurt her the way his father had hurt his mother, and part of him wondered if he'd ever truly be able to completely forgive himself.

The horn blared again, making them both jump.

"Go stall the cab driver," she said, before reaching up and pressing a quick kiss to his cheek.

His hand shot up to where her lips had skimmed his skin.

"What was that for?"

Penny giggled, a noise he hadn't heard in years.

"For taking me out dancing."

Daniel shook his head slowly from side to side.

"Wait until you've seen me dancing before you thank me," he said with a laugh.

"I don't care," she said, walking backwards into

the kitchen. "Just the thought of it's enough to make me smile."

Daniel followed her with his eyes before heading out the door. There had been times he'd wondered if he would ever get his life back. If he'd ever emerge from the darkness that had surrounded him these past few months.

What he had now was hope.

A hope that they might emerge on the right side of the emotional hell they'd been through this year.

# CHAPTER TWELVE

PENNY stepped out of the cab, conscious of Daniel behind her. His hand fitted against the small of her back when he emerged from the vehicle, softly propelling her forward.

"No way."

Daniel's arm encircled her waist. A voice of doubt in her head told her to shrug it away, to move sideways slightly to force his arm to fall, but she ignored those instincts.

She braved a look up at him. He rememberd alright.

Pushing him away now was hardly being fair to what she'd promised.

"You remember when we first came here?" he asked.

"How could I forget?"

They passed the security on the door and she let herself be led inside.

"The only difference is that last time we were both asked for identification at the door."

Daniel pulled her closer again as they made their way toward the bar. A band was playing and the music was loud, so his mouth moved close to her ear so he could be heard.

She could feel the heat of his breath against her cheek.

"And the music was a little different, too."

She laughed. "Are we that old?"

He shook his head. "Nope. We were just really young back then."

People surrounded them, and Penny hated it. Her role in the army had made her suspicious, made her look at situations differently. It would take a long time for her to become a civilian again, in the truest sense of the word.

"Wasn't the night we came here…" Oh. She'd spoken before she'd thought it through.

Daniel's fingers moved against her waist, enough for her to know that he'd heard her.

She braved a look up at him and saw the look in his eyes.

He remembered all right.

"If I recall correctly, you stayed over at my place."

Heat hit her cheeks. That was a polite way of putting it.

He tugged her a bit closer as he secured a place at the bar, ready to order their drinks.

"And we didn't spend a night apart until you had to leave for training."

Amazing. "I can't believe you remember," she said.

He touched the back of his finger to her cheek before answering. "I can't believe you thought I'd forget."

The bartender leaned toward them and Daniel ordered them champagne.

"I thought you only drank beer?" Penny nudged him in the ribs.

"What, you think I'm some Neanderthal who can't drink anything but lager?"

Penny had forgotten how good it felt to have sore cheeks from smiling too much. "Yeah, actually I did."

He gave her what she guessed was his fiercest look. "We had it the other night to celebrate your homecoming."

"Only because your mother would have killed you for saying no to it."

He paid for their drinks and passed her one, before holding his little finger out at an angle and taking a sip of his.

"Fancy enough for you?"

She tried not to laugh at him. "Seriously, Daniel, if that was your toughest look before, I'm glad you never tried to make it in the army."

He spluttered, choking on his next mouthful.

"Are we seriously going to have this conversation?" he asked, one eyebrow raised.

Penny groaned. "Don't even try to give me your navy versus army spiel, because everyone knows it's not true."

"Navy is tougher than army any day of the week," he announced.

Penny leaned her back against the bar and enjoyed another sip of the bubble-infused drink.

She'd forgotten what good company Daniel was. It had been so long since they'd had time to be like this. The two of them, with no work commitments keeping them apart, without Gabby, just the two of them.

"Do you guys even go to the gym?"

"You've answered the question yourself," he said with a smirk.

Penny had a feeling she was falling into a trap but she didn't get it. Now it was her with her eyebrows raised in question.

*"Guys,"* he said, drawing the word out. "I hate to say it, Pen, but there were no girls on my team. I think we both know which sex is the stronger one."

She set her glass down, arms folded over her chest. "Oh, no, you didn't."

He shrugged, but the grin on his face said it all. He knew he was in big trouble.

"Come on, Pen, admit it. You'll never beat a boy in an arm wrestle." He was smirking at her. She knew he was teasing but he had her riled.

"Well, a *boy* would never beat *me* when it came to strategy."

Daniel threw his head back and laughed. "God, I've missed this," he said when he came up for air.

Penny tried to stay fierce, to keep her game face on, but his smile cracked her frown.

She held out her hand. "Truce?"

He put down his glass and reached for her palm, tucking his against it, intertwining their fingers.

"You know I was only kidding, right?"

She narrowed her eyes. "No man will ever own up to the fact that a woman could be tougher than him."

"Is it so wrong for me to want to protect you? To pretend that you need me in your corner to keep you safe?"

The softness of his tone made her sigh. "No, there's nothing wrong with that, Daniel."

Truth be told, she loved that he wanted to be her protector. When she was away, everything rode on her own shoulders. Every decision, every tactic, every operation she was involved in. She had to be as tough as the guys, as smart as anyone else out there, and when she was leading others, it wasn't only herself she was trying to keep safe.

But at home, she'd always liked that Daniel was tough enough and strong enough to be a real man in a situation. When she came home for good, she wanted to leave her training at the front door and just be a woman in need of a man for once.

Penny gulped. Was she already presuming

she'd be coming home to Daniel? That they could repair the cracks and make *them* work again?

"Do you remember what you were wearing that night we first came here?"

Penny gave in to Daniel's touch and enjoyed the sensation of his skin on hers. The way his chocolate-brown eyes focused on her made her feel like the only woman in the room.

"No, but I remember why I came here with you," she said, thinking back to that night. "Because you made me feel like there was no one else you'd rather be with, that I was the most important person in the world when you were talking to me."

"You were wearing a leather skirt and a silky top," he said, leaning in close. "And heels that almost made me choke on my drink when you walked in."

Penny tilted her head back. "That skirt was *way* too short. My roommate made me wear it."

Daniel's index finger stroked the top of her hand. "I wasn't complaining."

The music was loud and the crowd was getting more intense. Penny found herself pressed up against Daniel as someone bumped her from behind.

His chest was firm as her hand slid between them to push back slightly. Penny was light-headed and it had nothing to do with the half-glass of champagne she'd downed.

"Want to head outside?"

She nodded.

Daniel gripped her hand tight and led her through the people surrounding them. No one stood in his way, and she liked it, tucked behind him as he moved.

Even though she was respected by her unit and superiors, size wasn't what made her tough. It was her mind and her attitude that had seen her succeed, not the fact that a crowd would part if she put on a tough face and strode ahead.

Daniel, on the other hand, had the brains *and* the brawn.

Cool air hit her face as she stepped out the door behind him.

"That's better."

Daniel kept leading her, out onto the patio and to the far corner where there were fewer people.

"It never used to be this packed full of people ten years ago."

Daniel's face was suddenly serious.

She took a step toward him that stopped as the band finished their song and the place was silent.

"We could have stayed inside after all if they're taking a break for a while."

Daniel shook his head, reached for her glass, and set both of them on the low ledge nearby. He returned and took her hands in his.

"Listen," he said, the word little more than a breath of air.

"Daniel…" He held one finger to her lips to stop her from talking, then turned her around, toward the bar from where they'd come.

Daniel pulled her back against his chest, so she was leaning into him. "Listen," he whispered again.

"We've had a request for a different kind of song this evening," said the lead singer, voice gravelly, the microphone squeaking as he spoke to the crowd. "I've been reliably informed that it's a firm favorite. An oldie but a goody."

Penny shut her eyes, her body at peace

against Daniel's, immersed in the music of their special song.

She'd never imagined he would even remember the littlest of details. But he did. He *had*.

His lips touched the back of her head before he murmured to her.

"Do you want to dance?"

She bit down on her bottom lip, resisted the urge to grin at him.

"You sure know how to make a girl feel remembered."

His hands traced across her shoulders then settled on her hips as she tucked her face into the hollow between his shoulder and collarbone.

"What I want is to make you feel loved."

That, too. He did make her feel loved. But she couldn't say it out aloud, wasn't ready to push her feelings that far.

Penny shrugged her thoughts away, refused to over-think the situation and let her body enjoy the moment while it lasted. They swayed, the gentlest of motions, the length of their bodies pressed together as they moved in time to the music.

Suddenly nothing else mattered. Nothing else

was important. Except for the slow music keeping their bodies touching, giving them an excuse to be so close they could have been one.

She'd never stopped loving Daniel, no matter how much she'd tried to think otherwise.

She'd never stopped wanting this, no matter how much she'd struggled, never stopped wishing they could step back in time and recover what they'd once had.

"And I'm free, free falling," Daniel murmured against her cheek.

She was, too. Falling so hard that she knew she'd never survive the drop if he wasn't there to catch her.

The song started to fade, the music stopping and being replaced by a louder, more modern song. She wondered what he'd done to convince the band to deviate and play it.

"Is it wrong that I want you to forget serving our country and stay home with me?"

Penny let her eyes slide shut again and pressed her cheek to Daniel's as he lowered his face.

"No," she whispered back. "It's not wrong. It's just…"

"How I feel about the woman I love."

Penny swallowed, too afraid to respond. She didn't want this moment to end. Didn't want to deal with the realities of what had happened, of what had torn them apart in the first place. Didn't want to think about what the coming months held.

What she wanted was to enjoy *now*.

"Spend the night with me, Penny."

Goose pimples rippled across her skin. She had a feeling he wasn't talking about sharing a bed and spending the night on opposite sides of the mattress.

"Daniel, I…" She what? She had no idea what she wanted, whether she was ready, but she *wanted to*. There was no denying that.

"What about Gabby? Your mother…"

"If we're not home by midnight she's staying the night anyway."

Oh, hell.

Could she do this?

"But…"

Daniel's hand slid down to her lower back, cupping her firmly, before tipping her back. His lips founds hers, crushing them, tasting her as he dipped her.

All thoughts fled Penny's brain. All she could think about was the feel of him beneath her fingers, the way his mouth teased so gently across hers. The pull of her mind, body and soul to his.

Daniel pulled away and she pushed her stomach in toward him, anchoring them together. She didn't need to ask him to know what he was thinking, what he wanted.

"What do you say?" he asked, dimple creasing as he smiled. The gentle, kind look in his eyes reassured her, told her she was safe with him. That she could say no and he wouldn't push her.

But *no* wasn't the answer she wanted to give him.

"Yes."

Daniel didn't need any further encouragement. He snaked his arm back around her waist and tugged her inside, not pausing this time to ask her if she was sure.

"Where are we going?" she asked.

"Somewhere we can walk to."

Penny looked down at her feet, then at him. "In these heels?"

Daniel placed a kiss on her cheek as they walked.

"No, not in those shoes."

He swept her up off her feet, making her feel lighter than a strip of cotton candy. His arms were firm around her, holding her tight to his chest, his grip strong.

"Better?"

Penny laughed. "I think you'd better put me down." Not that she wanted him to. Not that she wanted to take her head from his chest where it had fallen to rest, or give up the feeling of lightness, of feeling loved. "People are staring."

He stopped and put her carefully to her feet. "I don't care what people think, but your skirt's probably too short for being carried like that."

Penny's cheeks flushed as she grabbed at her hemline. "Daniel!"

He shrugged, but the smile caught her off guard and made her laugh all over again.

"Think of this as a trip down memory lane," he told her, eyes still smiling but his tone more serious. "We spent our first night…"

"At that little hotel a few blocks from here," she finished for him.

"Yeah." He bumped his hip into hers as they walked.

"What made you think of all this, Daniel?" she asked.

He stopped walking and caught her face in both of his hands, palms pressed to her cheeks.

"Because this is how we fell in love once, Penny. And I hoped it was how we'd fall in love again." His words were tender, heartfelt, and she couldn't ignore the way he was watching her.

Only she didn't know what to say in response.

But she did know what to do.

Penny stood on tiptoe and let her lips flutter over Daniel's. Tears prickled behind her eyes, but she denied them access. This was not the time to get emotional. It was time to think of nothing other than how Daniel was making her feel right now.

He took her hand in his and led her down the street.

Penny followed, numb with worry, yet with a tingling in her belly that told her she was doing the right thing.

# CHAPTER THIRTEEN

DANIEL'S body was thrumming with an energy he'd forgotten he could even possess. Penny's hand in his was soft, her body skimming his as they walked.

He'd wondered if he'd ever feel like this again, and right now it was as if his life was finally back on course again.

"Why don't you head over to the elevator and I'll collect the keys."

He saw a look he presumed was embarrassment cross her face. Daniel pulled her in tight and dropped a kiss on the top of her head.

"I have a room booked," he told her. "I did it just in case, and I didn't want you to feel embarrassed about walking in off the street."

Penny looked relieved. She would have hated to look like they'd just met and were spending the evening together, even to strangers, he knew that.

"Thank you."

Daniel collected the key card and joined her, letting Penny walk into the elevator ahead of him.

"You okay?" he asked.

Penny was nervous. He'd known her long enough to recognize it.

In fact, she looked terrified.

"Yeah," she said, but her voice was shaking. "I'm fine."

They stopped at their floor and stepped out. Daniel led the way and opened their door, standing back again to let her through first.

"Oh, Daniel!"

He saw the room only a moment after she did. Wow. It was beautiful.

"I thought, just on the off chance you wanted to spend the night together here, that I'd make it special."

Penny had tears in her eyes as she turned to him; her hand was covering her mouth.

"Is it too much?" Damn it! He thought she'd like it.

Penny shook her head. "It's not that, Daniel, it's…"

He went to take her hand, to comfort her, but she took a step back.

She looked bewildered as she surveyed the room again. The rose petals strewn over the bed, champagne and chocolates on the side table, a few candles flickering.

Penny pulled away from him.

"I need a minute."

Daniel's pulse started to race, but he tried not to let it show on his face. She was backing out, he could feel it.

"Take all the time you need."

Penny looked like she wanted to bolt. Like she was going to run for the bathroom then look for an escape route. Climb out the window or something, and never look back.

He hoped not.

She crossed the room and disappeared. Daniel sunk onto the bed, before thinking better of it and opening the bottle of champagne he had ordered earlier. Chilled and waiting for them.

The last thing he wanted was to get drunk, but right now he needed *something.*

Penny placed her hands on either side of the sink bowl and tried to catch her breath. Her heart was racing, palms clammy.

She couldn't do this.

Could she?

Daniel was her husband. The man she'd pledged to spend the rest of her life with. So why was this so hard?

Because all of a sudden she couldn't stop thinking about the fact that Daniel had seen another woman naked. That he'd been with someone other than her.

Would she measure up? Would he compare their bodies? Did he really even want her still?

Penny turned on the cold tap and let the cool water run over her wrists.

Was she being stupid?

Maybe she wasn't ready for this. But then if she wasn't now, would she ever be?

"Penny, you okay in there?"

Daniel's voice sent her heart beating into overdrive again.

"Just a minute," she called back.

But she needed longer than a minute. And she needed longer than the few days she had left before she had to leave.

It was too much pressure. Too…

"Penny?"

She stood tall, forcing her shoulders back, looking at herself in the mirror.

This was her chance to see if their marriage could be saved.

Perhaps her one chance.

It was now or never. No matter how she was feeling. No matter how nervous she was or how much Daniel's infidelity still haunted her.

"Penny?"

This time when he called, she opened the door.

Daniel hadn't realized he'd been holding his breath until the door opened and Penny emerged. His lungs suddenly felt like they were going to explode.

And he was nervous, too. Damn it, he was nervous like he hadn't been since he was a kid.

"Penny, I didn't mean to put pressure on you."

Her smile showed her nerves. "I'm okay, Daniel. I needed a moment to catch my breath, that's all."

Daniel waited for her to move toward him, but when she didn't he took hesitant, slow steps to her.

She didn't move. Her arms hung at her sides;

her eyes were on his but flickering, like she wasn't sure where to look or what to do.

"I know I told you earlier, Pen, but you look beautiful," he said. "Really, you do."

Her face was shy, cheeks flushed the softest shade of pink.

Daniel closed the space between them and raised a hand to her hair. He caressed a silky lock, all the way down to the small curl at the bottom.

"I've missed this."

Penny looked up, eyes hooded as she peeped from beneath dark lashes.

He shuffled closer, until their upper bodies were touching, so close he could feel the beat of her heart against him.

"The feel of you," he said, running his fingers through her hair again. "The smell of you." He dipped his face closer to hers, inhaled the sweet fragrance of her perfume. "The taste of you."

That time he paused, waited, gave her the chance to pull away.

But she didn't.

Penny's face, open and trusting, tilted upward. Her lower lip was trembling. She looked scared.

Daniel slowly placed a hand around her waist, the other still resting on her hair, fingers connected to each strand. He kissed her slowly, gently.

Her body was stiff, but only for a heartbeat. She molded against him, her body soft and supple.

"Danny," she murmured as he pulled back, kissing her one last time before pulling himself away. He walked backwards, holding each of her hands clasped in his.

"I love you, Penny." Daniel pulled her forward, linked her hands behind his back. "I love your nose," he said, before kissing the tip of it. "Your eyes." He ran a finger across her eyebrow then down the side of her face. "Your mouth."

She offered her mouth up in response, kissing him deeply, arms tracing their way from his back up to his neck, cupped behind his head.

Daniel took it as an invitation, trailed his own hands down her shoulders and to her back, feeling for the zipper on her dress and pulling it slowly down.

"I've missed this. Missed you," he murmured. She sighed and found his mouth, lips searching out his. Not wanting to talk, wanting only to touch.

But this wasn't just physical. Daniel wanted to talk. To tell her why he loved her, what he'd missed. To make sure she knew there was no one else who could ever make him feel like she did.

When he slid the zipper the entire way down, her dress fell, pooled on the ground at her feet.

Daniel stole his mouth from hers and kissed a slow trail down her body, starting at her neck and nibbling down her chest, hands lingering over her lace bra, lips searching out the skin on her belly then down her legs, until he was on his knees at her feet.

"Daniel," she protested, voice shaky, hands raised to cover her body.

"Don't even think about asking me to turn the lights out," he said, lifting first one of her high-heel-clad feet then the other so she could step out of the dress.

He straightened his body again and this time placed a hand on each of her shoulders, turning her until she stood with the bed behind her.

"When I tell you how beautiful you look, you can believe me," he told her, holding her gently, supporting her weight, as he tipped her back onto the bed.

Penny's eyes widened as he lifted his arms to pull his shirt off, before folding his own body down onto the bed, over hers.

Penny had never, ever felt so vulnerable.

She was trying so hard to stay calm, but her heart was racing and she was starting to panic. She couldn't shut her mind off.

"I want tonight to be perfect," he whispered.

Daniel lowered himself, resting on one elbow as he touched her face with one hand and started to kiss her again.

But he must have felt her stiffen, because his lips withdrew. The warmth of his face no longer against her own.

"Penny?"

It was as if her heart was cracking open, piece by tiny piece.

She couldn't go through with this.

Suddenly having him above her made her feel like she couldn't breathe, like she was being suffocated.

"Daniel, I need to get up," she said.

His brow creased, confused, but he didn't move.

"Now!" she said, louder this time.

He rolled sideways and she leaped off the bed, trying to cover her breasts. Feeling vulnerable, scared.

"I can't do this," she sobbed as tears clouded her vision. "I can't." Penny stumbled, looking for her dress, hating that she was so bare, in her underwear and heels.

Daniel was behind her, his hands on her hips.

"Don't touch me," she cried. "Please *don't*."

"I didn't mean to push you, Pen," Daniel said, voice low and apologetic. "Let's just sit here, let me hold you."

"Where's my dress!" She felt hysterical now. She needed to cover herself, to get out of here. Away from him. She couldn't do it, no matter how much she'd wanted to. No matter how badly she wanted them to work.

The candles, the champagne, the room…it was all too much pressure. Made her wonder if this was what he'd done with the other woman, even though he'd told her what had happened. Was it her he really wanted to be entertaining here? Would she even shape up?

"Don't go." Daniel's voice was flat, as if he knew there was nothing he could do to stop her.

She ignored him, ignored the intense pain within her body that made her feel like her heart was literally shattering into hundreds of tiny pieces. Ignored the pounding in her head, fought the words that wanted so desperately to be released.

Penny struggled into her dress, tears falling onto her bare arms.

She had to get out of here.

"I'm not letting you leave." Daniel's voice had lost the softness it had held earlier, and was now commanding. *Determined.* "Tonight is not ending like this."

She shook her head, not ready to fight. Not wanting to argue.

She didn't have the energy or will to take this out on Daniel any longer. She'd tried. Given it her best.

But in this case, her best was not good enough.

"Let me past, Daniel."

She had no idea how she was going to get home, what she was going to do, but she needed to be alone.

"No."

"Please." It came out as a sob, tears clogging her throat.

"I love you, Penny," he said, blocking her from getting through the door. "Do you still love me? Or don't you? Is that the problem here?"

A fresh wave of tears filled her eyes, but Penny angled her chin, forced herself to be brave. "I do love you, Daniel, that's never been our problem."

His face crumpled, there was no other way to describe it and she'd never seen such pain on another human being's face before. He knew what the problem was, and he hated himself for being the cause of it.

Just like she hated herself for not being able to move on from what he'd done, for not being able to forget. For failing him when he needed her, for not realizing that everything wasn't okay while she was away and pretending like it was.

"I can't block it out," she told him. "Every time you touch me, I think of you touching *her.* When I think about you making love to me, I wonder how I'll compare." They were the most honest, true words she'd ever spoken.

And also the hardest.

Penny touched Daniel's face with her open palm, cupped his cheek.

She loved him, she did.

"I can forgive you, Danny," she whispered, shaking her head from side to side, trying to shake off the emotion striking hot like an iron through her insides. "You were hurting and lonely, I understand that, I do. I hate what you did, but I will forgive you."

"But?" he asked, his dark brown eyes filled with the same big tears she could feel in her own.

"But I don't know how to forget, I can't do it," she said. "I've tried so hard, but I can't. I need more time."

They were both silent.

Penny wished she were angry, but it wasn't anger that was hurting her. That was holding her back.

"I need to go," she said.

Daniel's shoulders slumped forward. He ran a hand through his hair.

"I'll stay here, give you some space."

"Thank you."

Penny opened the door. "Goodbye, Daniel."

He didn't answer and she kept walking.

Daniel closed the door as gently as he could. His head was pounding, his hands were starting to shake, his body was rigid like it could snap with one wrong movement.

Damn it!

He wiped furiously at the tears crowding his eyes, willed them away. Looked around the room like a mad man waiting to strike out.

And he did. He couldn't contain his rage any longer.

Daniel reached for the bottle of champagne and threw it against the wall, jumping at the sound of it smashing. He reached for the glasses, hating everything about the room. About the perfect scene he'd tried to create.

He raised his arm to hurl his glass against the wall, too, but he couldn't do it.

A sob burst from his mouth, so loud it sounded as if it had come from a wild animal. A noise he didn't recognize.

Daniel dropped the glass at his feet before sinking onto the carpet beside it, knees hitting the floor.

Tears streaked down his cheeks and he didn't have the energy to wipe them away.

He knew the meaning of a broken heart now. Knew how the pain of one could kill a man.

Because right now, the pain he felt, the sense of sinking, of isolation, of gut-wrenching agony, was as real as if someone had stabbed a knife through his stomach and left him to bleed out.

He'd lost her. And there was nothing he could do to make things right.

In two days' time, she'd be gone.

His marriage was over and he had only himself to blame.

# CHAPTER FOURTEEN

PENNY'S eyes were sore and swollen from crying as she peeked into Gabby's room. The cab ride home from the hotel had been the longest drive of her life, made her feel so desperately alone she'd wanted to curl into the fetal position and never emerge.

But that wasn't an option for her. She was a mother and a soldier. She had to find the strength to continue, no matter how much pain she was in.

"Mommy?"

"Gabby?" She fumbled her way over to flick on the bedside lamp, not able to see clearly enough from the tiny sliver of light from the hall.

"Honey, what are you doing awake?"

Penny sat on the bed and stroked her hand through Gabby's hair.

"I had a bad dream," she said, tucking in tight against her mom. "Will you lie with me?"

Penny needed to touch, to hold Gabby, as much as Gabby needed her.

"Sure, honey, let me take my shoes off."

Penny flicked off her heels and kicked them to the ground, tucking her legs up on the bed and shuffling sideways to put her head on the pillow beside Gabby's.

"I can't wait for you to come home next time, Mommy," Gabby whispered, her tiny hands clasped between their faces.

Penny pushed the words away, not ready to deal with what it'd be like next time she came home. Not capable of thinking that far ahead, about what her future would be like.

About life without Daniel.

"Have I ever told you you're the most the important person in my life?"

Gabby snuggled closer again. "Even more special than Daddy?"

Penny bit down hard on the inside of her mouth, curled one of her feet into the other in an effort to keep her emotions at bay.

"Yeah, even more special than Daddy, because you're my baby girl."

"I love you as much as I love Daddy, even though you'll be gone again soon," Gabby said.

Penny couldn't help the sad smile that broke out on her face. All this time worrying that she'd ruined her relationship with her daughter by her absence, upset that she loved her father more than she loved her and that they'd never recover from it, for nothing.

"I love you, too. More than anything in the world."

Gabby stayed quiet, enveloped in her arms, breathing steadily but not yet sleepy.

"Go to sleep now, honey. I'll stay here with you."

Gabby didn't say anything, and Penny held her tight, leaning backward a smidge to turn the light off.

She wished things could have turned out differently, that she wasn't shedding tears over the fact her marriage was over.

But it was. And there was nothing she could do to change that.

Daniel had tried his hardest and she'd done her best to forgive and forget. In the end, it had all been too much.

Too much pressure with the hotel room and the champagne and the flowers. Too soon to be in that position. Too fast for her to make such a huge decision and decide whether they could ever move past this and be the Danny and Pen of old.

Gabby started to softly snore.

She had her daughter, and that's what she had to be thankful for.

She'd survived two terms serving her country, and she was healthy and whole.

Gabby's hair was wet against her cheek and it took Penny a moment to realize it was from her tears, that they'd fallen into Gabby's soft locks.

*Goodnight, baby girl,* she mouthed silently. *Sweet dreams.*

This was her second-to-last full night here. Then it was back to living in an army camp, wishing she was tucked up beside her daughter's tiny, warm body all over again.

Daniel strode through the door silently, but with a determination that he hadn't felt since he'd left the navy.

He'd lost it back there at the hotel, but he'd

pulled himself together and he knew what he had to do.

Daniel walked quietly down the hall, careful not to make a sound, and went through the open door into his bedroom. It was dark, and when he flicked the lamp on he saw that the bed was still made.

His heart started to pound.

Had she even come home?

Daniel hurried back down the hall, panic creeping into his mind. He pushed the door of Gabby's room open more fully and peeked in, but it was too dark to see.

He walked slowly, waiting for his eyes to adjust.

And when they did he saw a larger silhouette beside Gabby's small one.

"Penny?" He dipped his mouth close to her ear, not wanting to wake Gabby. "Penny?" He nudged her shoulder gently.

She stirred, then mumbled something he couldn't decipher.

"Pen, wake up."

He took her by the hand, giving her a gentle tug. Her eyes popped open, he could see them flash in the dark.

"Daniel?"

"Shh." He encouraged her to get up and she did, following him out into the hall.

The light there was only low level, and he didn't want to talk to her in hushed tones outside their daughter's bedroom.

"Daniel, what are you doing here?" her voice was a low hiss.

He beckoned for her to follow. "We need to talk."

She followed but he could tell from her pace alone before she even spoke that she was going to resist.

"We've said everything, Daniel. Please, let's not put ourselves through this again."

He held his tongue until they were in their bedroom and he could close the door behind them.

"Penny, can you sit down?" he asked.

She looked reluctant, but she sat on the edge of the bed. He did the same, taking a deep breath for courage before saying the words he needed to say. The words that had entered his mind, come to him, after he'd broken down in the hotel room. Too late to tell her before she left, but not too late to say now.

"Penny, I know you don't think you can forget, but the truth is, I can't either."

She looked uncomfortable, about to protest, but he launched into what he had to say before she could stop him.

Daniel took her hands in his, shuffled closer to her on the bed and looked into her eyes.

"I'll always remember your eyes, Penny Cartwright, for as long as I live," he said, willing her to listen, needing to tell her this for both of their sakes. "Do you know why?"

She moved her head ever so slowly from side to side.

Daniel touched his hand to the edge of her eye, stroking his thumb lightly over the skin there. "Because these were the eyes I looked into on our wedding day," he said gently. "The eyes that reassured me, without you needing to say a word, that I had nothing to be nervous about, that everything was going to be okay when we became man and wife."

He watched as her eyes misted over, knew that he'd hit enough of a nerve for her to keep listening.

He was telling her the truth, nothing more, and it was the right thing to do. Daniel could feel in his heart that it was what he needed to say. No matter what happened, he owed it to both of them to be honest, to tell her how he felt.

"I looked into your eyes when you lost your mother, and I wished I could take away the pain I saw there, but I knew that by looking at you, you'd know how much I loved you."

She reached to brush tears from her cheek, falling in a slow trickle.

"I'll never forget your eyes because I looked into them seconds after our daughter was born and saw a happiness there I'll never forget, and when you had to leave her to serve overseas, I'll never forget the pain I saw there either."

"Daniel…" She tried to stop him but he needed to say his fill, to get the words off his chest.

He moved his hand to her belly, resting it there.

"I'll never forget your stomach, Penny, because I stroked it every night once I arrived home from overseas, talking to our little girl. I'll never forget that you carried my child for nine months and made me the happiest man on the planet."

Penny was crying now, silently crying as she listened to him, but she never broke his gaze. Her lower lip was caught between her teeth, and it stayed there as he brushed his fingers across them.

"I'll never forget your lips because of the times they've kissed and reassured me." He tried to stop his voice from cracking as he said the next part. The hardest part. "And I'll never forget the way you reassured me that I'd never be like my father."

That made Penny shake her head, expression no longer sad, determined now.

"You're not your father, Daniel."

"No?" he asked. "I think I am, Penny. You gave me your trust and I stomped all over it."

It was Penny who touched his face then, who took over where he'd left off. "You're not like him, Daniel, because he hurt your mother on purpose. He *left her* and never came back."

Daniel sighed. "I hurt you, too, Penny, and I was unfaithful. That's enough to make me like him. But you're right, I'm different from him, because I want to make this right. No matter what, I want us to be okay."

She played with the hem of her dress, still wearing the same clothes she'd been in earlier.

"Penny, what I'm trying to say," Daniel said,

cupping her chin in his palm and lifting her head ever so slightly, "is that you might not be able to forget what I did, but what I can't forget is *you.* I know you might not believe me, but I never think of that night, other than to wish it didn't happen. All I remember is *you,* and how much I love you. How much I love everything about you, and wouldn't change a thing even if I could. How much I wish our life could be like it was."

"But—"

"You're my wife, Penny, and when you stand in front of me there's no one else I want."

They stared at one another.

"And I cannot imagine a life without you in it. I can't let this be the end, Penny. *We can't.* We mean too much to one another to just walk away."

Her lip trembled as she tilted her head higher. "Daniel?"

He nodded.

"Kiss me."

He moved slowly, pausing before taking her face in his hands and touching his lips to hers.

Penny's heart was thumping as Daniel's lips traced a path over hers. She couldn't deny the mellowness in her body, the pleasure of having his mouth covering hers.

Could she do this? Could she move forward and let him back in again?

*Yes.* Her mind was screaming out at her, forcing her to put aside her worries. *Yes.*

This, right now, *this* felt right. Being in some hotel room had seemed too forced, too staged. Had been sleazy somehow.

But being here, in their own room—hearing Daniel tell her how he truly felt—this was what she'd needed to believe in him again. To know that she was what and who he wanted, to know that she wasn't second best. That he'd never hurt her like that ever again.

"I love you, Penny. I always have and I always will."

She couldn't answer him, but she didn't pull away.

Daniel was right.

They could do this.

After everything he'd seen, the look on his face when he'd been so honest with her... She knew in her heart he was being honest. That he hadn't meant to hurt her. That she meant more to him than anyone else, than *anything* else.

"I love you, too, Daniel," she whispered. It seemed like forever ago since she'd been able to say that to him. To tell him how much she cared for him.

"Whatever happens, Pen," he told her, pulling back to caress her face, to talk to her, "I want you to know that you mean everything to me."

Penny let her head fall back, neck arched as he kissed her, like the tip of a feather being tickled across her skin.

Now she could forget.

Had forgotten. Had forced herself to.

Because Daniel was right. What they had been through together, what they had felt for one another in the past, what they'd created together, was more important than anything else.

And it meant they absolutely, truly deserved a second chance.

Daniel slipped the strap of her dress down over her shoulder, reached for the zip before hesitating.

"Love me, Danny," she whispered, shy yet bold at the same time.

His lips found hers again as she wriggled and he unzipped her from her dress.

This time she didn't pull away. Didn't panic. Because this time it felt right.

# CHAPTER FIFTEEN

DANIEL propped himself up on one elbow and looked down at Penny. It had been a long time since he'd felt like this. The past year had been rough, but things were finally feeling right again. Like they could make their marriage work again and be the family they used to be. The family they'd always wanted to be.

"Pen?"

He stroked the edge of his hand across her face, brushing her hair from her forehead to rest on the pillow.

"Yeah?" she murmured, eyes closed as he touched her.

Daniel reached for the bedside-table drawer and fingered the ring he had there. A pretty band inset with a modest row of diamonds that curved around the entire ring.

"Penny, I need you awake for this."

Her eyes opened, a lazy expression still resting on her face.

He tucked the ring under the pillow before she could see it and went back to touching her, stroking his hand down the curve of her back now as she wriggled closer.

"This is the first time in so long that I've been really happy, Penny," he told her, fighting to push out the words.

It didn't come naturally, talking about his feelings so openly, but this was his one chance. If he didn't open up to her now, it would be too late.

"I wish I knew how much you'd been struggling," Penny said to him, raising her own hand to trace across his cheek. "If I'd known how hard you were finding everything, if we'd been more honest with one another about how hard this was, then maybe..."

He tilted his head, eyes on hers.

"It's not your fault, Penny. None of this was your fault, and you don't ever have to worry about anything like that ever happening again. You know that, right? Because we're going to make this work."

She didn't need to respond. They'd both faced

their own battles, their own demons, this past year. But she trusted him. After all this, after what they'd been through and how they'd reconnected again, he knew in his heart that she would trust him. It wasn't going to be easy, but they were going to make this work.

"I asked you for a chance when you came home, Pen," he said, his voice so low it was almost a whisper. He inhaled deeply, stomach dancing with nerves.

She snuggled closer. "Thank you, Danny, thank you for making me believe in us again. I would never have forgiven myself if we'd never given us another shot."

"But?" he asked.

She raised her eyebrows. "Does there have to be a *but?*"

"No," he said with a laugh. "I was just so sure there'd be one."

Penny raised her head and whispered a kiss across his lips.

"What was that for?" he murmured against her mouth as she pulled back.

"For making me feel like me again," she said simply. "For making *us* right again."

She could have been talking for him. It was exactly how he felt. Like everything within him had finally realigned.

"We only have thirty-six hours left."

She flopped her head back down onto the pillow. "I know."

Daniel summoned every drop of bravery within him and slipped the ring out from beneath the pillow where he'd hidden it.

"Daniel?" She was suddenly alert again, eyes wide as she spied what he held.

"You haven't worn your wedding rings since you've been home, Penny…"

"I never should have taken them off." Penny looked as if she was going to cry.

He sat up properly, facing her on the bed. She did the same, legs crossed. Her hair was long and tumbling forward over her shoulders, long legs tanned and lean, peeking out from beneath lacy boy-shorts.

"You had every right to take them off," he told her, his left hand touching her knee. "And I want you to leave them here until you come home again."

He watched as she blinked away tears, confusion clear on her face.

"Why?"

He reached for her left hand and held out the ring he held before slipping it onto her finger.

"This ring symbolizes a promise, Penny, and I want you to wear this until you come home. If you want it."

She watched him without saying anything.

Daniel took both her hands in his. "I want to give you this ring as my promise to you, that I will forever be faithful to you," he said, voice low and crackly. He breathed deep. "I want you to be my wife, Pen, but I want to deserve that honor."

She nodded, one side of her mouth curving upward. "Thank you, Danny."

"For what?"

"For being the husband I always knew you could be."

He pulled her close, into his lap, wrapping his arms tight about her and wishing he'd never ever have to let her go.

"We can make this work, I know we can," he whispered against her hair.

Penny slipped her hands around his neck, pillowy lips raised to his, waiting to be kissed.

"I don't want to leave you," she said.

Daniel fought a choke as it built in his throat. Fought against the sadness and anger that filled his body at the thought of Penny leaving him. Leaving Gabby.

Tried to ignore the worry that niggled in his mind at the thought of her flying back into a situation that could prove so dangerous it could steal his wife from him.

"I'll be here for you when you get home. Us being okay, together, is the one thing you don't have to worry about while you're gone."

Penny rubbed her face into his shoulder, buried it against his chest.

"I love you, Danny. I love you so much I can hardly breathe."

"Me, too, sweetheart," he said, dropping a kiss to her forehead. "Me, too."

He felt the wetness of her tears against his chest, and hated that he was so powerless to take away her pain.

"I wish leaving weren't so hard."

"I know, baby, I know."

And he comforted her the only way he knew how. By holding her deep in his arms, lips to hers, and wishing he'd never have to let go.

"Why is it going to be different this time, Danny?"

He let his chin rest on the top of her head.

"Because we're going to talk, and tell each other when something's wrong or when we're struggling."

He listened to her sigh. "So no more being brave and acting like everything's okay when it's not."

Daniel dropped a kiss into her hair. "We need to talk as often as you can, and I'm going to keep a diary of what Gabby and I do every day. So you don't feel like you've missed out while you're away."

She grinned and looked up at him. "And you have to ask for help if you need it, okay? From your mom or Tom."

He groaned. "Not Tom."

"Okay, not Tom. But you need to speak up if things get tough. And when your boys are back, you need to hang out with them. Just like you need to make sure you keep up your air time."

Daniel stroked his thumb across Penny's cheek. "Why did we not have this conversation before you left last time?"

There was a dampness in her eyes. "Because we were so busy trying to pretend like everything was going to be okay, and we didn't want to admit that there could be cracks."

Daniel didn't have to think when Penny's lips found his. Instead, his body moved against hers, responding naturally like they'd never spent a night apart.

Penny being away was never going to be easy, but they were both committed to making it work, and that's all that mattered.

It's why he knew that they had a real chance at being happy and in love all over again. Stronger than before.

Penny fought to keep her chin high, shoulders squared. Unlike when she'd arrived, now she wore her army fatigues. And this time she'd let Gabby come with them.

Daniel had been right, it was silly to keep it from their daughter. She might only be five, but she had the right to be proud of her mother, deserved to know why they'd be parted for months again. Serving her country was something to be shouted from the rooftops, to be shared with Gabby. She'd been scared to tell her before in case it worried her, but she was too young to understand what could happen in a worst-case scenario.

Seeing her mother in uniform today had put a smile on Gabby's face, and anything that helped take the edge of pain off their parting today was worth it.

"Is there anything I can do?"

Penny shook her head and held Daniel's hand tighter.

"The last time you held my hand that tight you were giving birth to Gabby."

She sunk her head down onto his shoulder and tried to program the scent of him, the feel of him, into her memory bank.

"How do you always know how to make me smile?"

Daniel dipped down to hoist Gabby up, planting her on his hip before slinging an arm around Penny's shoulder.

"It seems like forever now, but we'll be together

soon," he said. "And we're going to talk and *write* this time, too, right?"

Penny cuddled into them both, bending forward to kiss Gabby. She wasn't going to say anything to the contrary, not while Gabby was listening. The last thing she wanted was to upset her when she was being so brave.

But personally, she was terrified. At the thought of leaving, at the worry of what had happened last time she'd been away. Whether she was strong enough to cope without her family, and whether they were strong enough to cope without her.

Daniel bent to put Gabby back down and pulled his camera from his pocket.

"Can I take a snap of my two girls?"

Penny wanted to say no, because she was feeling too fragile to do anything other than have both Daniel and Gabby by her side until she had to board. But she also wanted Gabby to have a permanent memory of this day. Of seeing her mother off at the airport before she headed off for her final tour of duty.

Daniel stepped back, half crouched to take the shot.

"Excuse me?"

They all looked over at a woman who'd stopped behind Daniel.

"Would you like me to take a photo of all of you?"

Daniel gave her one of his trademark beamers, dimple shining out, before passing her the camera.

"Thank you," he said.

Penny smiled her thanks to the stranger, too, before falling into Daniel's embrace at the same time as he scooped Gabby back up into his arms.

The flash went off but Penny found it hard to let Daniel go.

"You make a beautiful family," said the woman.

Penny looked up at Daniel and reached for her daughter. The love she saw in his gaze, shining out from his eyes, made the breath sigh from her lungs.

They did make a beautiful family.

Now she just needed to summon the strength to cope with leaving them, and look forward to the day they'd be reunited. Because they would make this work. It wasn't going to be easy, it was still going to be tough, but they *would* work through it.

Penny fingered the new ring she wore around her neck on a platinum chain.

Daniel had promised to be here for her. And with every beat of her heart, with every pump of blood through her veins, she believed him. Because he was her husband and she had to have faith.

"We're going to miss you," he whispered.

"I know," she murmured back. "But when I get back, it's the start of our new life together."

Daniel tucked a strand of hair that had fallen from her braid back behind her ear.

"Only four months, three days and eighteen hours until we'll be waiting here again, right?"

Penny tilted her head back and laughed.

"I'll take your word for it."

Daniel put Gabby back down and engulfed her in a bear hug.

"You're the one, Penny. You always were, and you will always be."

She kissed him as he dipped his head to find her mouth.

"I love you," she whispered.

"I love you, too," he said. "Now go board that plane and hurry home, okay?"

She dropped to her knees to kiss her daughter goodbye.

"See you soon, hon. I love you so much."

Gabby looked sad, but relaxed into her father's legs as he stood behind her and wrapped his hands around her.

Penny stood up, gave them a salute and hauled her bag over her shoulder.

She forced herself to walk, to keep her legs moving without looking back.

But when she reached the departure gate, she couldn't help herself.

Penny pivoted, bag still over her shoulder, and let her eyes wander to where she'd left Daniel and Gabby.

They were still there, watching her back.

Penny raised her hand in a brave wave and burst into a tearful laugh as Daniel blew her a kiss.

*Four months, three days and eighteen hours.*

And then they'd all be together again.

But right now, she needed to board that plane and serve her country.

# EPILOGUE

PENNY fidgeted as she waited to walk through security. She was starting to panic.

She knew they'd be waiting. Daniel had written to her constantly while she was away, and they'd been able to talk almost every four days this time, but she was still worried.

Because now her army days were over. Now she was home forever.

Everything they'd talked about, everything they'd promised one another, was about to become reality *now*.

The security officer waved her through and she walked faster than she ever had in her life. The airport was busier this time than last, but she didn't care. There were two faces she was looking for and she wasn't going to stop until she saw them.

"Penny!"

The deep, booming voice that reached out to

her stopped Penny in her tracks, heart beating so hard she was in danger of a heart attack.

Daniel.

She would know his call, the sexy richness of his voice, anywhere.

Heat flooded her cheeks as she looked around, eyes searching frantically.

And then she saw him. Gabby was running along beside him as his long legs ate up the ground.

"Penny!"

This was it. This was the homecoming she'd been waiting for.

She smiled so hard she wondered how her cheeks didn't split, but she didn't have time to think about it. Before she could bend to see Gabby, Daniel had hold of her, swinging her up into his arms as if she weighed no more than a newborn baby.

"Hey, soldier," he whispered, before skimming his lips across hers.

Penny sighed into his mouth, arms caught up around his shoulders.

"Hey to you, too."

"Do you have any idea how much we've missed

you?" Daniel's eyes were glued on hers, pupils the color of the richest dark chocolate.

"Yeah, we've missed you heaps, Mommy," said a soft voice laced with shyness.

Penny snuggled her face into Daniel's chest for a heartbeat, craving his touch, breathing in the scent of him, loving feeling like a featherweight in his arms.

But she wanted Gabby in her arms just as bad.

She reluctantly wriggled from Daniel's grip and bent to throw her arms around Gabby. "However much you missed me, honey, I missed you a whole heap more."

Gabby shook her head and looked at her feet. But she held her wrist, adorned with the charm bracelet, up at the same time. Shy.

"Daddy told me to take this off for school but I never did," she said.

Tears flooded Penny's eyes but she did her best to blink them away as she fished in her carry bag.

"I bought this for you while I was away."

Gabby looked up, eyes bright. "But it's not even my birthday yet."

Penny looked at Daniel and saw that his eyes had misted up, too.

"This is just for being special," she told her daughter, holding out a little box with a bow around it.

"Shall we head home?" Daniel asked, reaching for Penny to pull her to her feet, other arm circling Gabby's shoulders.

"Yeah," she said, beaming up at him. "I can't think of anything better than going home.

"Daddy said he's going to take you up in a helicopter tomorrow," Gabby said, wriggling the bow off her present as they walked.

"Oh, really?" Penny thumped Daniel on the arm. "That's funny, because Daddy knows how much I hate flying."

Daniel shrugged, grinning even as she thumped him again. Gabby laughed, wide-eyed.

"He said it was a special occasion, so you wouldn't be able to say no."

"Daniel…" Penny tried to protest.

He grabbed her hand, spun her around and scooped her up. Gabby squealed and ran in front of them.

"Don't you dare put me over your shoulder, Daniel Cartwright!" she insisted.

"Do it, Daddy! Do it!"

Penny was laughing so hard she couldn't even fight him.

"Say yes, Penny," he ordered. "Say yes to the helicopter ride or I'll carry you all the way to the car."

She wriggled one more time then gave up.

"Yes!" She laughed. "I surrender!"

"Good," said Daniel, dropping her back to her feet.

But she couldn't scold him. Not when he wrapped both arms around her and bent her backwards for a kiss that tingled all the way to her toes.

A round of applause broke out and Gabby opened her eyes as they straightened.

She'd forgotten she was still in her army fatigues. That there were other people around them.

Penny's cheeks flushed but Daniel responded with a bow before grabbing her hand and Gabby's.

"Come on, girls, let's go home."

Penny had no intention of protesting when it came to that particular request.

\* \* \*

The helicopter moved with a steady beat into the sky. Penny kept her eyes shut. Tight.

"You can look," Daniel told her.

She could tell without peeking that he was smiling. That he had stolen his gaze from where he should be looking, and he had turned his aviator-glasses-clad eyes toward her. That his too-cute dimple was grinning her way.

Penny shook her head. No.

"I can't believe in all these years that you've never been up with me."

"You know I hate flying, Daniel."

He chuckled. "Says the girl who's just flown halfway around the world for the second time in four months."

Not funny. He knew what she meant.

"It's magical, Pen. Please look," he pleaded.

She sucked back air like she was on the verge of hyperventilating.

It wasn't that long ago that she'd seen a Black Hawk go down over the desert, and she hated having to go up in the sky.

"Penny?"

"Okay."

She peeled one eyelid slowly back, then the other.

And her heart stuttered before kicking back into gear again.

*It was amazing.*

Daniel's laugh made her look at him.

"Thank you."

She didn't know if he'd heard her whisper through the headset, but she couldn't make her voice any louder. The breath had literally been stolen from her lungs.

"You're not serving now, Pen. This is just me and you."

She tipped her head back until it rested on the seat and looked through the wide windscreen.

"Where are we going?" she asked, confidence slowly trickling back through her body.

Daniel didn't answer straightaway, leaving her to gaze out the window and watch the world disappear beneath them.

"You might not like surprises, Pen, but this is one thing you're going to have to wait to see."

She bit her lip to keep her mouth from breaking into a big grin. Part of her wanted to cry. To sob out loud and let all her emotions out. Being home was so surreal she could hardly describe it. Dealing with the fact that she was never going to have to leave her family again.

Penny lifted her arm up, relinquishing her grip on the helicopter's door. Her childhood charm bracelet rested on her wrist, tiny charms swaying as she flexed her fingers.

When she'd seen Gabby wearing hers at the airport, she'd felt a sudden desire to wear her own, to remember her own mom. Now, high above the air, *free,* it seemed right.

"Prepare for landing."

Already? "I was just starting to enjoy myself."

Daniel didn't divert his eyes but she saw his dimple crease. "We'll be back in the air again before you know it."

Penny let her fingers drop back to the door, but her knuckles didn't turn white this time. Her body was still relaxed, shoulders not tense like they had been when they'd made their ascent.

"I know you're going to laugh at me, but it's really nice being up in the air with you, Danny. I have to admit it," she told him.

His focus remained fixed on flying. "Tell me

that again once we've landed. I want to look you in the eye and make sure you're not kidding."

Wow.

Penny hardly heard his last words. Her hand flew to her mouth.

The field below them was covered in wildflowers, bright colors that seemed to never end.

"Where are we?"

Daniel didn't answer her. He brought the chopper down slowly, hovering until they touched down carefully on the ground. He flicked a switch to cut the rotors, then removed his headset.

"You like it?"

Did she like it? Hell, yes!

"Daniel, I don't..." She shook her head in disbelief. "How did you know about this place?"

He grinned before jumping out and running around to open her door. He held out both his hands and she slid into his open palms as he reached to guide her out.

"The farmer produces honey and he has this field sown in wildflowers for the bees to pollinate."

Penny no longer cared how he knew the landowner or how he'd found the place. She didn't even want to look at the pretty field of flowers.

All she wanted was to stay in Daniel's arms. To stay in the one place in the world she felt safe and loved.

He took one of her hands and led her away from the helicopter, giving her a look she couldn't decipher over his shoulder as they walked.

"So about enjoying that ride?"

Penny swatted at his shoulder. "You need to hear it again, huh?"

"Sure do."

She twirled into Daniel as his arms engulfed her waist.

"You're an amazing pilot, Daniel," she told him honestly. "I should have trusted you sooner and gone up with you."

His eyes twinkled, but there was a seriousness there she couldn't figure out.

Daniel stepped back, holding her hands, trailing to her fingertips, before letting go.

"What's wrong?" she asked, worry licking like fire across her skin, making goose pimples appear on her bare forearms.

He looked solemn, reached for her hand again. Just the left one this time. Before dropping it.

"Daniel?"

Daniel looked down at the ground, then met her gaze. Without breaking eye contact, he reached for her necklace and unclipped it. Took it gently from around her neck.

She held her breath as he slid the ring off the chain and held it up.

"When I gave you this ring, I made a promise to you, Penny. That I would be faithful to you while you were away. That I would prove that we could make this work."

She nodded, tears in her eyes. He took her right hand and slid the ring on. She didn't resist, just stood there, motionless, incapable of words.

Then he dropped her right hand and reached for her left, his other hand disappearing into his pocket.

"Penny, I love you, and I don't want you to wear a promise ring around your neck anymore." He paused, the corner of his mouth tilting up into a smile. "I want you to be my wife again. To wear the rings I gave you on our wedding day."

She laughed. Penny actually laughed at him.

Until she saw the worried look on his face.

"Yes," she whispered, drawing him in, her mouth against his neck as she tucked her body into his. "Yes, Daniel. Yes!"

He pushed her back, his eyes full of questions, or maybe disbelief.

Penny held out her left hand to him and let him slide the rings home.

"Will you be my wife again, Penny? From today and for every other day of our lives?"

She nodded and pulled him back in for a deep kiss, lips pressed against his, arms around his neck and hands at the back of his head to stop him from getting away.

She released his mouth to whisper to him.

"Yes, Danny," she said. "Yes to everything."

In a field of wildflowers, with only the helicopter for company, Penny let herself be held and slowly folded down to the ground. Daniel's body molded snug against her, as if it was made to fit. Her hands touched along his muscled neck and shoulders, down his arms.

"What about the bees?" she asked as he traced a feather-light trail of kisses down her chest.

"To hell with the bees," he murmured.

Penny shut her eyes as Daniel's mouth covered hers again.

This was the homecoming she'd wanted. Her daughter safe at home, her husband in her arms, and their whole lives, *together,* before them.

\* \* \* \* \*